Lily Takes A Chance

Praise for the 'Lissadell' series

'A thoroughly enjoyable read and sure to become
a favourite in Irish households.'

Children's Books Ireland

'This historical setting, giving an insight into social-class
division, makes the Lissadell series among her most
accomplished yet.'

Evening Echo

Other Books by Judi Curtin

The Lissadell series
Lily at Lissadell
Lily Steps Up
Lily's Dream

The 'Molly & Beth' series
Time After Time
Stand By Me
You've Got A Friend

The 'Alice & Megan' series
Alice Next Door
Alice Again
Don't Ask Alice
Alice in the Middle
Bonjour Alice
Alice & Megan Forever
Alice to the Rescue
Viva Alice!
Alice & Megan's Cookbook

The 'Eva' Series
Eva's Journey
Eva's Holiday
Leave it to Eva
Eva and the Hidden Diary
Only Eva

See If I Care (with Róisín Meaney)

Judi Curtin

Lily Takes A Chance

a Lissadell Story

THE O'BRIEN PRESS
DUBLIN

First published in 2022 by
The O'Brien Press Ltd,
12 Terenure Road East, Rathgar,
Dublin 6, D06 HD27 Ireland.
Tel: +353 1 4923333; Fax: +353 1 4922777
E-mail: books@obrien.ie
Website: obrien.ie

The O'Brien Press is a member of Publishing Ireland
ISBN: 978-1-78849-392-5
Text © copyright Judi Curtin 2022
The moral rights of the author have been asserted
Copyright for typesetting, layout, editing, design
© The O'Brien Press Ltd

1 3 5 7 8 6 4 2
22 24 25 23

Internal illustration, cover design and cover illustration by Rachel Corcoran.
Photo credits: p 306: source unknown; p 308: courtesy of Judi Curtin; p 310: Alamy; used
with permission. Every effort has been made to trace holders of copyright material,
but if any infringement of copyright has inadvertently occured, the publishers ask the
copyright-holders to contact them.

Internal design by Emma Byrne.
Printed and bound by Nørhaven Paperback A/S, Denmark.

Published in

This book is dedicated to my lovely parents who both

died while I was working on the Lily series.

Thank you for loving and supporting me always.

I miss you.

Chapter One

'**D**id you hear the great news, Lily?'

I hurried towards my friend and put down my bucket, sloshing warm soapy water all over the floor.

'Please say we're getting a day off?' I said. 'Or a half day – even an hour would do me. I think I'll die if I have to clean another floor or make another bed.'

'Sorry,' said Nellie, using her mop to clean up the mess I'd made. 'It's not time off, but it *is* good news all the same. Lady Mary's got a huge, big bag of wool for us, and it's navy blue – isn't that great? It will be a lovely change for the soldiers.'

For months now we'd been knitting socks and vests for the poor young soldiers who were fighting across the sea in France and Belgium, and while I *was* fed up of the grey wool we'd been using, I'd been hoping for better news than that.

'Aren't you happy?' asked Nellie. 'Lady Mary said she'll send the wool to our room later so we can get started tonight.'

Nellie was so sweet and kind, and never sought anything for herself. All she wanted was to be a house-maid at Lissadell forever. That wasn't enough for me, though. I loved my friends, but I found the days long and boring. Sometimes my dream of being a teacher seemed so far away I might never, ever reach it – but as I looked into my friend's shining blue eyes, I had to smile back at her.

'I'm happy that you're happy,' I said. 'But don't you sometimes …?'

I stopped talking as I heard footsteps coming up the servants' stairs.

'It's Mrs Bailey!' said Nellie in a panic, starting to mop furiously.

Even though Nellie never did anything wrong, she was a bit afraid of the housekeeper, who was strict, but kind and fair.

The steps came closer, but when the door opened it wasn't Mrs Bailey.

'Lily!' said Maeve, rushing towards me. 'There you are, I've been looking everywhere. I've missed you *so much.*'

'Oh, Maeve, I've missed you too,' I said. This was true. Maeve de Markievicz was a young lady and part of the family who owned Lissadell House. Mostly she lived with her grandmother, Gaga, in a house called Ardeevin. She missed her father who lived abroad, and her mother, Countess Markievicz, who lived in Dublin. Maeve loved adventure and excitement and when she visited Lissadell everything seemed brighter and much more fun.

'Oh, hello, Nellie,' said Maeve then. 'How are you?'

'Hello, Miss Maeve,' said Nellie politely. 'I'm fine, thank you. How are you?'

I sighed. My friends were very different, and no matter how hard they tried, I knew they would never be friends with each other.

'I'm going to see Star, the pony,' said Maeve. 'Would you like to come, Lily?'

I preferred most things to mopping floors, so that wasn't a hard question. Unfortunately, though, I couldn't always do what I liked. I had a job, and responsibilities.

'I've already talked to Mrs Bailey, and she said you can come,' continued Maeve, as if she'd read my mind. I wasn't supposed to be doing things like this, but all the servants loved Maeve, and bent lots of rules to make her happy.

I turned to Nellie, who, I knew, would end up doing some of the work I was leaving behind.

'Go,' she said. 'There's not much to do here. I'll sing to myself, and the time will fly.'

'Thanks, Nellie,' I said. 'I'll make it up later, I promise.' Then I skipped after Maeve, feeling free and happy.

* * *

When we got to the stables there was no sign of Teddy, the groom.

'Hello?' said Maeve. 'Is anyone here?'

A boy came out of one of the storerooms. His face was covered in golden freckles, and his untidy, curly hair was the colour of fresh straw.

He stared at us, and I wondered what he thought of Maeve in her gorgeous dress and dainty shoes, and me in my servant's apron and heavy boots. We were a strange pair to be arriving at the stables in the middle of the morning.

'Hello, Miss …?' he said. He was smiling, and not a bit embarrassed the way my little brothers Denis and Jimmy are when they meet strangers.

'I'm Miss Maeve,' said Maeve.

'And Miss …?' he said, looking at me.

'I'm Lily. Just plain Lily.'

'I'm Sam,' he said. 'Today is my first day. Teddy's gone on a message. Can I help you with anything?'

'We'd like to see Star,' said Maeve.

So, the three of us went to Star's stable, chatting as we went.

We stroked the pony, and Maeve gave her the carrot she'd brought.

'I can saddle her up if you'd like to go for a spin,' said Sam.

'We can if you like,' said Maeve, turning to me.

I'd ridden Star once before and loved it, but changing into riding clothes would take ages, and I couldn't stop thinking about Nellie, stuck inside doing endless jobs on her own.

'No,' I said. 'You go if you want.'

'It's no fun on my own,' she said. 'Come on, I'll walk you back to the house.'

* * *

I thought about Sam as we walked.

I liked the twinkle in his eye, as if he thought everything could have a funny side if only you looked hard enough.

I liked the way he could easily see how different my position was from Maeve's and yet he still treated us the same.

'Sam is nice,' I said.

'I suppose he is.'

Maeve was always polite to the servants, but except for me, she never paid any of them much attention. In a funny way, that made me feel good, as if I were special to her.

'Are you staying long?' I asked, almost afraid to hear the answer.

'Just a few days. Then I must go back to Ardeevin for more stupid lessons with stupid Miss Clayton.'

She was being funny, but still I felt a small bit jealous. I was never given a choice about leaving school, and I'd have loved a private governess, and the opportunity to spend the whole day reading books.

'Miss Clayton is being so mean,' Maeve continued. 'She makes me work very hard all the time, as if I were some kind of slave. She seems to think ...'

Then she stopped herself. 'Sorry, Lily. I know you work much harder than I do.'

I smiled. When Maeve and I first became friends, she never seemed to understand how hard servants had to work – and once we even had a big fight about it. Maeve had never walked in my heavy leather boots, and I'd never taken a step in her pretty silk shoes. Neither of us could really imagine what the other's life was like. Nowadays though, we were both trying hard, and getting better at understanding each other.

'It's all right,' I said, and it was.

'Miss Clayton was so annoying yesterday, I …'

'Oh no,' I said when she hesitated. 'What did you do?'

'I might have … well … I suppose I *did* deliberately knock over a bottle of ink, and some of it accidentally splashed on Miss Clayton's skirt. I didn't mean *that* to happen, but she was very cross, because she wears that skirt every day, so she must really love it.'

I smiled to myself. Some things would probably never change. Maeve would never understand that

working people wear the same clothes every day, not because they love them, but because they don't have any others.

'And some drops of ink got on Miss Clayton's shoes as well,' she continued. 'I said she should wear them like that – she might start a new fashion. I was honestly trying to be helpful, but I don't think she saw it that way.

'And then what happened?' I asked.

'Oh, I said I was sorry, lots of times, but that didn't help. Miss Clayton was in a big huff and luckily Albert came to bring me here, so I didn't have to listen to her for too long. But if she tells Gaga …'

'And *will* she tell on you?'

'She can't tell yet anyway, because Gaga left on a visit to some distant cousins yesterday morning.'

'And when Gaga comes back?'

'A normal person would forget what I did, but Miss Clayton has a very long memory. She probably will tell.'

'And then?'

'Gaga will tell Mother, and Mother will threaten to send me to England to boarding school – and if she does that ... oh Lily, my life will be over.'

I looked at my friend, who'd never spent a day at school in her whole life. 'You know, Maeve,' I said. 'School isn't such a bad place. I loved the lessons, and I had lots of friends. I was very sad when I had to leave and come to work here.'

'I know,' she sighed. 'I'm sorry you had to leave a place you loved – but for me, things will be so different. I'll have to go all the way to England, and I'll have to stay there for months and months, and never see you or Gaga or anyone else. I'll miss Star, and the dogs and the kittens and even my little cousins. I won't know any of the girls at school. Maybe they won't like me. Maybe they'll be mean to me.'

'Maybe they will love you,' I said. 'In fact, I'm sure they will – just like I do.'

She gave a small smile. 'But maybe they won't. I'll

cry myself to sleep at night, and no one will even care. Oh Lily, I don't want to go away.'

'Don't girls like … well, rich girls like you – don't you *have* to go to school at some stage?'

'Yes. I know I'll have to go when I'm much older – but I don't want to leave for ages and ages, maybe even a couple of years. By then I'll nearly be grown-up, and I won't mind so much. By then you'll be gone away, and working as a teacher.'

I smiled at her. Glad she remembered my dream. Glad she was so sure it was going to come true.

'Then let's hope Miss Clayton doesn't tell on you,' I said. 'Now walk faster, or I'll be in trouble with Mrs Bailey.'

Chapter Two

'I hardly make any mistakes these days,' said Nellie that evening as we sat on our beds. 'Soon I'll be as good at knitting as you are, Lily.'

'Soon you'll be much better than me,' I said, smiling at her. 'You've got more patience, and you don't get cross and rip everything back in a temper when you do something wrong.'

She didn't answer, but the touch of pink in her cheeks showed me she was pleased. Poor Nellie learned to knit when she was living in a workhouse, and the cruel teacher whacked her fingers with a stick every time she dropped a stitch. It was a wonder the poor girl could even pick up a pair of needles without crying.

The door opened and Johanna slipped inside. 'Room for one more on that bed, Nellie? I've brought

my own needles.'

Nellie beamed at her big sister, and slid closer to the wall. She adored Johanna, and would have made room even if it meant *she* had to sit on the hard cold floor.

Johanna made herself comfortable, and for a few minutes the only sound was the click of our needles, the crackle of the fire in the grate, and Nellie's gentle humming. It was very cosy and peaceful, and it was hard to imagine that in Europe, there was a terrible war going on.

'Will Harry be back to work soon?' I asked. Harry was a footman at Lissadell, and he was also walking out with Johanna. He'd just come back from the war with terrible injuries to his face. He wanted to give up his job, but Sir Josslyn, who owned Lissadell, wouldn't hear of it.

As usual, Johanna smiled at the mention of Harry's name. 'It's going to be another little while. Sir Josslyn has arranged for him to go to Dublin. He's getting

a special mask made, to hide the worst of his scars.'

'Harry's scars *were* frightening the first time I saw him,' I said. 'But after a few minutes, I stopped noticing and he was just the usual old Harry.'

'Lily's right,' said Nellie. 'Why does Harry even need a special mask? Maybe people who don't like looking at scars should get special glasses so they don't see them.'

'That's nice of you, girls,' said Johanna. 'To me, he's as handsome as ever – and I will love him no matter what happens – but he won't listen. He thinks his face will scare visitors to Lissadell, and that's why he's agreed to let Sir Josslyn help him with the mask.'

'Sir Josslyn is a kind man,' said Nellie. 'Now we should be kind and get on with our knitting. There's lots of poor soldiers in Europe with very cold feet!'

Harry had told us a bit about what life at war was like – and it sounded terrible. The soldiers spent days at a time in trenches, which were often filled with water, and their feet were always cold. Warm socks

like the ones we were knitting could save them from a horrible disease called trench foot.

I picked up my knitting with a sigh. Women weren't allowed to fight, so we had to help in any way we could.

* * *

'I need someone to run an errand,' said Mrs Bailey next day, coming into the drawing room where Nellie and I were dusting the glass cases of dead butterflies and beetles.

'I'll do it,' I said, dropping my duster.

'You're very keen, Lily,' said Mrs Bailey. 'Since you don't even know what the errand is.'

I didn't care what the errand was. Sometimes I felt like the poor butterflies, pinned to paper, trapped under glass, never free to fly in the fresh, clean air.

'I'm only trying to be helpful,' I said primly. Nellie gave a snort of laughter, and I had to turn my head

so Mrs Bailey wouldn't see that I was laughing too.

'Indeed,' she said. 'Now take this note and bring it to the head gardener, and don't dilly-dally.'

'Yes, Mrs Bailey,' I said, and skipped out of the room. Free at last!

* * *

I ran all the way to the greenhouses, and luckily the gardener was there, so I didn't have to waste time looking for him. That meant I could walk slowly back, savouring my few minutes out of doors.

I strolled along, enjoying the sweet singing of the birds in the trees, and the crunch of my boots on the gravel. I held my head high, pretending I was a fine lady, going to a big party where I'd eat the best of food, and swish my silk and satin skirt as I danced with my rich friends.

The imaginary party vanished into the air as I heard footsteps behind me. I jumped when I felt the

touch of a hand on my shoulder.

Was this one of the Gore-Booths?

Was I in trouble, even though I hadn't done anything wrong?

But it wasn't a Gore-Booth. It was Sam, with a huge smile on his face.

'What are you looking so happy about?' I asked in a mean voice. I was embarrassed, as if he could somehow read my mind – could tell what silly imaginings had been running round my head.

'I'm just glad to see you,' he said. He pretended to look hurt, but his eyes were twinkling in a way that made me smile.

'Sorry. I'm glad to see you too. How are you getting on – now that you've been here at Lissadell for two whole days?'

'I like it. Everyone is very nice to me. I enjoy being around the horses, and the food is the best I've ever had – last night Cook sent us some left-over custard tarts and they tasted like something that came

straight from heaven, but ...'

'But what?'

'Here is good, but it's not where I want to be.'

For a second I couldn't answer. Never before had someone described so exactly the way I felt.

'What *do* you want?' I asked, when I finally found my voice.

'I want to join the army. I want to go to Europe and fight. I want adventure. I want excitement. I want army pay, which is so much better than what I get here.'

I knew you had to be eighteen to join the army – (I'd checked ages ago, and was very relieved that by the time my little brothers were old enough, the war would surely be over).

'But you're too young to join up!'

'How dare you say that! I *am* old enough. I'm actually a very small and skinny eighteen-year-old.'

I felt my cheeks going red. 'I'm very sorry, Sam. I thought ...'

'I'm teasing you,' he said with a big laugh. 'I'm not eighteen – and won't be for another couple of years. If I were eighteen, I wouldn't be here, and that's for sure. I'm not going to let my age stop me though. As soon as I can find a way, I'll be in uniform and gone far away out of here.'

'But how?'

'Don't you worry about that. If you want something badly enough, there's always a way to make it happen. Now, much as I'm enjoying standing here with you, I think we might both lose our jobs if we don't get back to work. May I walk you to the house?'

'Thank you,' I said, and we started to walk, not very fast, as if we both wanted to make the chat last.

'And what about you?' he asked. 'Do you like it here at Lissadell? Would you like to stay in this fine place for the rest of your life?'

'I *do* like it. I've got lots of friends and the Gore-Booths are kind people, but ...'

I had so much to say, but I hardly knew this boy.

Why would he want to hear all about me?

'Go on,' he said, sounding interested. 'Tell me the rest.'

'The work is so boring. Every single day is the same. My friend Nellie loves it like that, but I can't bear it. For a while it was better. For a while I spent one day a week in the sewing school and sometimes I did lessons with little Michael and Hugh Gore-Booth.'

'And you liked that?'

'I *loved* that, but now they don't need me in the sewing school, and Michael and Hugh have a tutor, so it's back to endless cleaning for me.'

'My mam loves cleaning. She does it all the time – even when the place is hardly dirty at all.'

'My mam too, but I hate it so much. I work very hard to make a room nice, and then it gets messed up, and then I do it again and again and again. Every single day.'

Sam broke a twig from the tree we were passing. 'If this were a magic wand, and I could give you any-

thing at all, Lily – what would you wish for?'

'That's easy! I'd wish to be a teacher in my old school, where I used to go before I came here. The Master would teach the big children, and I'd teach the small ones, and I'd like that because they're very sweet. And some days I'd teach knitting and sewing and singing to the big girls too – and I'd be kind to them all, not like Miss O'Brien who was mean to anyone who wasn't good at sewing.'

'Miss O'Brien doesn't sound very nice. Would you have to work with her?'

'No. The school is only big enough for two teachers. Miss O'Brien is engaged to be married to a man from Donegal, and the Master says when she leaves, I can go and work as a Junior Assistant Mistress in her place – and I wouldn't need any training or anything. That's important, because Mam could never afford to send me to training college.'

'Well, that's sorted then. Can we do anything to make Miss O'Brien hurry up and get married?'

'It's not that simple. She could take years and years to make up her mind. Once she brought a bottle of milk and one of water for her lunch, and all the kids laughed as they watched her picking up one, and then the other, trying to decide which to drink. By the time she decided, the Master was ringing the bell for us to go back to our lessons.'

'That's funny – and waiting must be hard, but if you're patient, your wish will come true sooner or later.'

'That's the trouble – I'm afraid it won't. There were lots of clever girls coming up behind me in the school. By the time Miss O'Brien leaves, the Master might want to give the job to someone else.'

'Ah, but he probably won't. And where will you live, when you're a teacher?'

I wanted to hug him for saying 'when' instead of 'if'.

'At first, I'd live with Mam, and help her with my little brothers and sisters, and after a few years when

they're grown up a bit, I'd have my own little house, but still near Mam so we could go for walks every day when our work is done. And in my house I'd be in charge of everything, and I'd make it nice, and I wouldn't mind cleaning because it would be all mine.'

Sam stopped walking and so did I. He waved the twig in the air over my head. 'Close your eyes and make your wish,' he whispered.

I felt a bit silly, but he looked very serious and hopeful, so I did as he said.

'Nothing's changed,' I said as I opened my eyes. I couldn't help feeling disappointed, even though I'm too big to believe in wishes and magic wands. 'I'm still here. My wish isn't coming true.'

'You don't know that.' Sam laughed as he threw the stick into the hedge. 'All you know is that it hasn't come true *yet*!'

'You're funny,' I said.

'I can be serious too though. I listen when people are talking. I can see that the world is changing.'

'Changing how?'

'This life – one rich family being waited on by all these servants, that's not going to last.'

'I'm not sure you're right,' I said.

'Trust me, I am. Things were changing anyway, and the war will make everything happen faster. You wait and see. Soon young girls like you won't want to live in basements of big houses and work all day long. Girls will move to the city and work in shops and offices and factories. They'll earn more money and have more freedom. Women like Mrs Bailey will want their own lives, with children and independence. People are going to expect more than they have now – and that's not a bad thing.'

I knew some people liked things the way they were, and would've been cross to hear Sam talking like that – but I couldn't help feeling excited at the idea of a different world. I thought of my school friend Hanora, who was now working in a shop in New York, and living the life Sam was describing. Could

that really happen here in Ireland?

It was getting late, so we ran the rest of the way back. Sam waved when we got to the stables.

'See you, Lily,' he called as he hurried away.

'See you,' I said, already feeling sad.

I wanted Sam's wish for me to come true, but what about his wish for himself?

What if he found a way to join the army?

I knew already this boy was going to be my friend – what would I do if he went away to that terrible, cruel war?

Chapter Three

'I've only got half an hour, Maeve,' I said as the two of us walked towards the stables. 'And then I've got to be back to help Nellie beat the drawing room carpets.'

Maeve gave a big sigh. 'I wish you didn't have to work. Without work you and I could have such fun together.'

'I wish that even more than you do, I promise,' I said. 'Now walk faster or it'll be time to go back before we get there.'

Star was a beautiful pony, and she nuzzled my hand as I fed her the pieces of turnip we'd brought. 'You're the most beautiful girl ever,' I said, as I stroked her nose, and felt her warm, straw-scented breath on my cheek.

'Sir Josslyn says you need to ride her more often,

Miss Maeve,' said Teddy the groom, coming along the cobbles with a bucket of feed. 'Or else she'll be out of practice when Master Michael is big enough to take her out. If you want to go now, I can have her saddled up in a few minutes. I have everything ready.'

Maeve turned to me. 'We could both go out on her – take turns!'

'No,' I said. 'I haven't got time, but you go if you like.'

'I'd prefer to do something with you,' she said. 'But I don't want to make Uncle Joss and Aunt Mary angry. I might need them when …'

She didn't finish, but I knew what she meant. If Gaga wanted her to go away to school, Maeve was going to need some grown-ups on her side. She was a determined girl, but that might not be enough.

So, five minutes later, Maeve, was seated on the pony, looking very elegant in the riding clothes she kept in a room over the stables.

'I'll talk to Mrs Bailey,' she said. 'And maybe next

time you can ride too. Or on your day off you could borrow Star and ride her home.'

What would Sir Josslyn think if he heard I was riding around the countryside on the pony he'd bought for his precious children?

What would they say in my village, if I showed up on a finer creature than even the richest families could dream of?

Poor Teddy looked as if he was going to faint away at the very thought of it.

'I think maybe I'll borrow your bicycle as usual, Maeve, if you don't mind,' I said.

'As you wish,' she said. Then she clicked her heels and Teddy ran to keep up as Star trotted towards the woods.

I began to walk towards the main house, but then stopped myself. I wasn't expected back for another while, so I might as well relax and enjoy myself. If anyone asked what I was doing, I could say I was waiting for Maeve.

I wandered to the small shed where the cats lived, hoping there might be a new litter of kittens.

'Oh!' I said, startled, when I opened the door and saw Sam sitting on the straw with one tiny white kitten in his arms, one crawling up his leg, and another peeping out of his jacket pocket.

'Shhh,' he said. 'Don't tell Teddy. I did my morning's jobs very quickly, so now I have a few minutes to play with these little beauties.'

'That's lucky. I've got a few minutes too. Now don't be greedy, and give me one of those babies.'

We chatted easily as we played with the kittens, and laughed at their antics.

'I brought you something,' I said after a while.

I pulled a custard tart from the pocket of my apron and handed it to him. It was a bit squashed, but he didn't seem to mind. He took a bite, and a slow smile spread across his face.

'That's so kind of you, Lily,' he said. 'Thank you.'

I felt embarrassed at how pleased he was, and

words began to pour out of my mouth. 'It's noth-ing ... when Maeve told me we could come here to see Star I had to run downstairs to put my mop and bucket away. I saw the tarts cooling in the kitchen ... and when Cook saw me staring, she said I could have one. I nearly took a bite, and then I remembered you'd said that ... and I thought I might see you near the stables and ... so ...'

Sam broke the remains of the tart in two and handed me the bigger piece. 'Plenty for both of us.'

I chewed my tart, wondering what to say next. It's hard when you've got a new friend, and you don't really know them well, but you want them to like you anyway, and you're afraid of saying something stupid that will make them laugh at you. Then I remem-bered one of Mam's sayings – *be yourself and you can't go wrong.*

'My sisters love kittens,' I said. 'They're very cute – my sisters I mean – but kittens are cute too.'

'You're funny, Lily,' Sam said, but not in a mean

way. 'Tell me about the rest of your family.'

So, I told him about my daddy who died, and my mam who worked so hard to mind us all, and how my wages were such a big help to her. I told him about my brothers, Denis and Jimmy, and my darling little sisters Winnie and Anne, and how they loved my visits home, and how excited they got when Cook gave me a basket of food for them.

Sam seemed really interested and asked lots of questions, but I knew I was talking too much.

'And what about you?' I asked. 'What family have you got?'

'There's Mam and Daddy. Mam is mostly quiet, but when she's angry – oh, Lily, you wouldn't want to cross her – she'd frighten the life out of you, but she doesn't mean a word of it really – I think. Daddy works on a farm. He wanted to join up, but he's got a gammy leg after a cow kicked him, so the army wouldn't take him – and he wasn't very happy about that. Then there's my two big brothers – they've

joined up already and they're both in Europe some-where. Daddy's very proud of them, and that's why …'

'There's other ways of making your daddy proud,' I said quietly.

'Maybe there are, but the army's the one for me.'

'You don't know Harry, the footman, do you?' I asked.

'No. Who is he – and what's he got to do with this?'

'Harry's my friend. You don't know him, because he's not working at the moment. He's in Dublin get-ting a mask made to cover the terrible injuries he got in the war.'

'He shouldn't wear a mask,' said Sam defiantly. 'He should be proud of his injuries! They show he was a brave man, fighting for what he believed in.'

'Harry *is* a brave man, but still, the things he saw and heard, they were so terrible. When he was injured, he was sent to a special hospital for men with injuries to their faces. He said there wasn't a single mirror in

the whole hospital.'

'But why …?' I watched Sam's face change, as he understood.

'Oh, Sam. War is so terrible. It's …' I stopped talking as I felt tears rush to my eyes.

Sam noticed and spoke more gently. 'I'm sorry about what happened to Harry, but I was born under a lucky star, and nothing bad will happen to me.'

'But how would you even be allowed to sign up? You're not old enough.'

'I hear there's a recruiting office not far away where they don't ask young lads like me too many questions.'

'What do you mean?'

'The recruiting officers don't care how old you are. One silly boy told them he was sixteen, and they told him to go for a walk for an hour, and be nineteen when he came back.'

I didn't answer, not knowing whether to laugh or cry at Sam's story.

'When my day off comes,' he continued. 'I'm going to borrow Teddy's bicycle and go see for myself. There's a war on, Lily and I'm missing it.'

* * *

As I made my way towards the house, I kept thinking back to when Harry left for the war. I remembered how afraid Johanna and Nellie and I were. I remembered the letters Harry sent us, telling us about the cold, and the dirt, about how afraid he was all the time. I remembered how he looked when he came back – so sick and pale, with only one eye able to see, with those scars that must have hurt him so much. I understand that men have to fight for what they believe in, but Sam was only a boy, and he was my friend, and he hadn't even left and already I was afraid of what might happen to him.

Chapter Four

I was getting used to cycling on cobbles, but even so, I was careful as I made my way across the coach house courtyard towards the gate. I didn't want to spoil my precious day off by falling and breaking my head open.

'Hey, Lily – look at you like a fancy lady!'

It was Sam, hurrying towards me.

'Hello, Sam,' I said, wobbling as I stopped the bicycle.

'That basket looks very full,' he said.

He was right. Cook was a kind woman, and as usual the basket was piled with good things to eat.

Suddenly I felt guilty.

Was Sam asking me to give him something?

Did he think I was selfish, cycling away with a huge basket of food on the front of my bicycle?

Friends were supposed to share, weren't they?

I didn't mind sharing my own food with Sam, but anything that came from the basket was coming from the mouths of my brothers and sisters, and my mam, who ate like a bird and always left the best things for everyone else.

I put my hand on the spotless clean cloth that Cook had used to cover the basket.

'I'm sorry, Sam,' I said, embarrassed. 'I'd like to share with you but ...'

Now he looked embarrassed too. 'No – I wasn't asking you to give me something. I'm only after having the biggest breakfast of my life and couldn't eat another scrap. I was wondering if you had room in your basket for something else?'

'Like what?'

He pulled his hand from his pocket and shyly produced the most darling wood carving of a kitten. It was tiny and sweet and perfect.

'You said your sisters like kittens, and I like carving

things, and there's lots of wood lying around here, so …'

I took the carving and ran my fingers along the smooth wood. 'Winnie and Anne will love it,' I said. This was true, but I also knew they would fight like two little cats over who would hold it first, and who would play with it, and who would sleep with it in their warm, curled fingers.

Now Sam took a hand from his other pocket, and showed me a second kitten, exactly like the first.

'I made two,' he said. 'Because you said the girls fight sometimes. And look, I carved a small *A* on the base of one, and a *W* on the other so they won't get mixed up.'

'Oh, Sam, thank you,' I whispered, unable to say any more. I loved that he'd taken the trouble to make two carvings, but more than that, I loved that he'd listened to me, and paid attention when I was talking about my family.

'It's nothing,' he said. 'Carving keeps me busy

when my work is done. I don't know if your brothers are too big for things like that, but if they're not, I ...'

'I couldn't ask you to ...'

'You're not asking, I'm offering, and that's a completely different thing.'

'Well ... they've both gone mad on wild animals like bears and tigers and lions and things. They read about them in a book at school ... and ...'

'Consider it done. I'll have them for you next week. Now I'd better go before Teddy comes calling for me. See you soon.'

'Yes, see you soon,' I said. 'And thank you – the girls will be so happy.' Then I waved as I got back on the bicycle, and set off for my favourite day of the week.

* * *

For once in their lives, Winnie and Anne were speechless. They took the little cats from me, and stroked and petted them as if they were real. A huge

tear rolled down Winnie's cheek, but I knew it was a happy tear. Mam put her arm around me, and we smiled at the little ones, and everything was perfect.

Denis and Jimmy came in from playing, and when they'd finished rooting through the basket of food, they paid attention to their little sisters who were still fussing over their new toys.

'Stupid toys,' muttered Jimmy, but his face was sad. Anything that came from Lissadell House seemed almost magical to my brothers and sisters, and I could see he was jealous.

'Don't worry, Jim,' I said. 'Next week …'

I'd already told Mam about the toys for the boys, and now she shook her head at me. 'Don't say a word, pet,' she whispered in my ear. 'Let the girls have their moment, and next week the boys can have their big surprise. It's best that way.

As usual, Mam was right. The boys helped to lay out some of Cook's treats for dinner, and the six of us sat around the little table, and as we chatted and

laughed it was like the old days when we all lived together, and we were happy as ever.

* * *

As always, the day went much too quickly, and before I knew it, I was cycling out of the village, back towards Lissadell. Now my basket was empty, except for a pair of woolly gloves Mam had given me as a present for Sam, to thank him for the toys.

'Don't let Denis see,' she'd said as she quickly wrapped them in brown paper. 'They were supposed to be for his birthday next week.'

'But …'

'Don't worry,' she said. 'I've plenty wool left, and I'll have another pair made in no time.'

* * *

I couldn't help feeling sad as I came to my old school. I stopped cycling and looked over the stone wall and

across the yard. I could hardly remember what it was like being a pupil there, and sometimes going back as a teacher seemed like a silly, childish dream.

Why couldn't I be more like Nellie?

Why couldn't I be happy with all the good things in my life?

Why did I always have to be dreaming of what might be impossible?

Suddenly the big door at the front of the school opened and the Master stepped outside. I'd been staring and now I was embarrassed. I wanted to duck down behind the wall, but if he saw me do that …

'Lily Brennan? Is that you?'

The Master always said he had eyes in the back of his head, and sometimes that seemed true. If I'd given in and ducked down, I'd have been so ashamed, I'd have had to crawl out of the village and never return again.

'Hello, Sir,' I said. 'Yes, it is me. It's Lily.'

By now he'd used the huge brass key to lock the

door, and was walking towards me.

'And how are things up at the big house?'

I couldn't complain. Life is hard for everyone, and I didn't want the Master to think I was a big, dissatisfied baby. He wouldn't want to work with someone who was always giving out. So I gave him a huge smile.

'Life at Lissadell is good, Sir,' I said. 'And everyone is kind to me. They feed us very well, and I have lots of lovely friends. I'm a lucky girl to have such a fine job.'

'So you don't want to be a teacher anymore?'

'Oh, no! … I mean yes. I do want to be a teacher – I want it more than anything in the world – well, I'd like if the war stopped and all our boys got home safely – but as well as that I'd like to be a teacher. I'd love to be with the little children all day. I'd still love to …'

He put his hand up to stop me.

'I think I understand what you're saying, Lily – and

I'd still like to have you working with me as an Assistant Mistress. I know you'll be a big success.'

'But Miss O'Brien?'

'Oh, she's dragging her heels a bit, I'm afraid. She has always been a cautious person, and now with the war, no one knows what to do any more.'

'So it could be ages and ages?'

'Well, she wouldn't want to leave it too long. Her young man might get tired of waiting, and she wouldn't like that. You just be patient, Lily, and work hard at Lissadell.'

'Of course I'll work hard at Lissadell – I haven't got a choice about that, but why?'

'Before you can be appointed, you'll need to get a good reference. I've known you and your family since you were a baby, and that's good enough for me, but the education board has rules that have to be followed. They will need to see a reference from your employers – in writing.'

'I'll work hard,' I said. 'I'll work harder than ever.

I won't let you down, Sir, I promise. When the time comes, I'll bring you the best reference that was ever written, you just wait and see.'

He laughed. 'That won't surprise me at all,' he said. 'You've always been a good girl. Now I must go, or my tea will be getting cold. Off you go, and be careful on that bicycle – when you're a teacher you'll need to be in the full of your health.'

I sang all the way back to Lissadell, and lots of people stopped to stare, and some little boys ran after me saying I sounded like a big hoarse crow, and I only laughed. I was still going to be a teacher and that was all that mattered.

* * *

'You look very happy, Lily,' said Nellie that night as we got ready for bed. 'Usually you're sad after your day off, but tonight you're … different.'

I smiled at her. Nellie didn't always say a lot, but she

noticed everything. But then, all of a sudden, I didn't want to tell her about my meeting with the Master. She was my friend, and I knew I could trust her, but I couldn't help being afraid. I thought about what the Master had said. I thought about Sam waving his magic wand. Maybe my dream was like the seeds of a dandelion – if I wasn't careful it might vanish in the wind.

* * *

For the next few days, I worked as I had never worked before. I polished and cleaned until my back ached and my hands were stinging. Whenever Mrs Bailey needed someone to do something, I was the first to jump up, even if it was a dirty horrible job no one else wanted to do.

On the third day, after I'd volunteered to clean up a mess one of the dogs had made in Sir Josslyn's study, Mrs Bailey looked at me strangely.

'Are you all right, Lily?' she asked.

'I'm perfectly fine, thank you, Mrs Bailey. Why do you ask?'

She narrowed her eyes, as if to see me better.

'I'm not sure, Lily. You've always been a good worker, but these days you're … how can I put it … you're … unusually perky.'

'I'm only trying to do my job, Mrs Bailey,' I said primly.

'Hmmmm,' she said, and I could see she wasn't convinced. 'Very well. Now run along. Sir Josslyn is ringing the bell again.'

Upstairs, I hummed as I cleaned up the smelly mess. One day I was going to be a teacher, and my days as a housemaid would be ancient history.

Chapter Five

'**H**ey Lily,' called Sam a few days later, as I was walking back from the apple store with a basket of wrinkly old fruit. 'Can you come for a walk? There's something I want to tell you.'

'Just let me give these apples to Cook,' I said. 'And then I can sneak a few minutes before my dinner. Wait here.'

I raced inside, gave the apples to Cook, then ran to my room, got the gloves for Sam and slipped them into the pocket of my apron.

'I've got ten minutes,' I said when I got back to Sam. 'Or fifteen if I don't mind Mr Kilgallon giving me cross looks all through dinnertime.'

'Let's make it fifteen, then – our lovely butler always looks a bit cross, so it shouldn't make any dif-ference.'

I laughed. He was right – Mr Kilgallon did always look a bit cross, but he was a kind man too, so I wasn't scared of him – most of the time.

'I haven't seen you since your day off,' said Sam as we began to stroll along the path.

'Sorry. I've been working extra-hard these days, and I haven't had a free minute.'

'Why? Are there visitors expected?'

'No – it's not that. It's …' And then, without really meaning to, I told him everything the Master had said, and how hopeful I felt. As the words tumbled out, I felt a bit guilty. I hadn't told Nellie, who'd been my friend for ages, so why was I telling this boy who I'd just met?

Then, as Sam's eyes sparkled, and as he jumped up and down with joy at my news, I understood why I was telling him. He had a dream too, so I knew he'd understand.

And then I remembered. 'You said you had something to tell me.'

Now Sam's eyes sparkled even more. 'I do. But it's a secret, so you have to promise to keep it to yourself.'

'Do I look like a tattle-tale?'

'I'm serious, Lily. You mustn't tell anyone. Do you promise?'

And so, because I really wanted to hear what he had to say, I quickly said. 'Yes. Yes, Sam, I promise.'

'I had the day off yesterday, so I borrowed Teddy's bicycle, and cycled to my friend Martin's house – it's not too far from here. And then I took him on the bar of the bicycle, to that place he'd told me about where the recruiting officers aren't fussy about details like how old you are. And you couldn't believe it, Lily, it was so easy. It makes sense though – Martin and I are tough out, so they could see we'd be good at fighting. They hardly asked us anything at all, and then we signed the papers they gave us, and we were in!'

I stared at him, not sure what to say. He was telling me what he thought was great news, and all I

wanted to do was cry like a baby. It wasn't fair that anyone had to fight, but especially not young boys like Sam, especially not boys who were my friend. I had so many questions, I didn't know where to start.

'But …' I muttered. 'There are rules about signing up … and you're not old enough … and …'

'There's a war on Lily, and some rules need to be broken.'

'If you've signed up, why are you still here?'

'They're going to ship us to England for training, but not for a few weeks. Until then, I can work away here, and Martin can stay on at school.'

Now I wanted to cry again. What kind of a world was it where schoolboys were sent away to fight?

'You shouldn't go!' I said. 'Neither of you should go until you're old enough.'

Sam didn't answer, and then I thought of something else.

'What did your Mam and Dad say about you joining up?'

'Nothing.'

'Nothing?'

'They couldn't say anything because I didn't tell them. Daddy will be proud when he hears the news, but Mam will probably kill me.'

'You're going to war,' I said bitterly. 'She might not have to kill you.'

For a second, he didn't look so chirpy, but then he brightened again. 'Mam wasn't happy about my brothers going to fight, but in the end she couldn't do anything about it.'

'The poor woman,' I said, thinking about my own mam, and how she'd cry if Denis or Jimmy went off to fight. 'When are you going to tell her?'

Suddenly he looked very young, and I could imagine the cheeky little boy he used to be. I remembered him telling me how cross his Mam sometimes got, and I had the funny idea that he was more afraid of her than he was of the enemy soldiers.

'I'll write to tell her when I get to England.'

'You *have* to tell her before you leave. You *have* to give her a chance to say goodbye.'

'You mean a chance to grab me by the ear and drag me down to the recruiting station? A chance to tell them my real age, and embarrass me in front of all the soldiers? No way, Lily. It's all settled. Mam and Daddy can't know until it's too late for them to do anything about it. I'll tell them in a letter, and there's an end of it.'

In the distance I could hear the sound of the servants' dinner bell.

I had to go.

But how could I go?

How could I leave this lovely boy with his stupid plan that might very well get himself and his friend killed?

'You can't do this, Sam. You can't.'

'Too late, Lily. It's done. I know you don't like the idea, but there's nothing you can do about it.'

This wasn't true. The recruiting officers might have

ignored any suspicion that Sam was under-age, but if I actually went and stood in front of them and told them the truth, they'd have to listen. If they knew the truth, they couldn't send Sam away to fight.

But it was as if Sam could read my mind. 'You said you'd keep my secret, Lily. You can't tell anyone – you *promised*.'

Why did I ever make that stupid promise?

Did I have to keep it?

Was it wrong to stay quiet, if a young boy was going to end up in battle? He might be injured, or even killed. He might never come home to Ireland again.

So what was I supposed to do?

'It'll be all right, Lily,' he said. 'We'll win the war, and save the Belgians.'

'I *know* the Belgians need help. I even met some of the refugees when Lady Mary took me to Sligo Town – but that doesn't mean that boys like you and Martin ...'

'I'll be back before you know it – probably even before those little white kittens are grown.'

I didn't trust myself to say another word.

The bell rang again. I didn't care about dinner. I didn't care about anything except the thought of this lovely boy going to battle. But I was too cross and sad and upset to hear any more. I turned away and headed towards the house.

'I'm not going for a few weeks, remember?' he called after me. 'I'll see you tomorrow?'

I didn't answer as I started to run, trying to take comfort from the clattering of my boots on the gravel, and the whoosh of the cold wind on my face. But it didn't help. Nothing could help.

'You're late, Lily,' said Mr Kilgallon sternly, as I breathlessly took my usual place at the table, next to Nellie.

I stared at him, barely conscious of the tears that were starting to run down my cheeks. Mr Kilgallon saw the tears, and his face softened a little. 'Try to be

on time tomorrow,' he said, but not in a cross way.

As people sat down and began to eat, they stopped staring at me. Johanna smiled from across the table, but that didn't make me feel any better.

'Lily,' whispered Nellie, putting her arm around me. 'What's wrong? What's happened?'

I tried to smile, but didn't succeed.

'I'm your friend,' she said. 'Whatever it is, you can tell me.'

But I couldn't tell anyone – I was going to have to figure it out all on my own.

Nellie patted my arm. 'Well, when you're ready to tell,' she said. 'You know I'll be ready to listen. Now take out your hanky and wipe your eyes and eat up your dinner.'

But when I reached into my apron pocket for my hanky, I found the gloves Mam had given me for Sam, and as I touched the soft wool, my tears began again.

* * *

That night, I couldn't concentrate on my knitting, and kept dropping stitches and forgetting where to increase and decrease. In the end, I threw my needles and wool at the wall.

Johanna ran to pick it up, while Nellie came and put her arms around me.

'Lily, pet,' she said, stroking my hair and wiping my tears with her hanky. 'What is it? Why are you so sad today? Is it your Mam or your brothers or sisters? Did you have bad news?'

I shook my head. 'They're all fine.'

'Then what? Did you have another falling-out with Miss Maeve?'

Once again I shook my head.

Now Johanna was sitting beside me too, holding my messy knitting on her lap. My good friends loved me, but I couldn't tell them the truth.

'Are you worried about the news from the war?' asked Johanna.

This was close enough to the truth, so finally I

nodded. My two friends patted me and said sweet things, and did their best to comfort me. In the end, I tried to smile, as I took my knitting from Johanna.

'I'd better get on with this,' I said as brightly as I could. 'Some soldier will need these socks to keep his feet warm in the trenches.'

The girls moved back to Nellie's bed and went on with their knitting. I looked at the half-made sock in my hand and hoped that Sam wouldn't be the soldier who'd end up wearing it.

Chapter Six

Next day I worked as hard as I ever did. The good reference for the Master was lurking somewhere in my mind, but also the heavy work distracted me from thinking about Sam.

I was just finished making up the bed in Gaga's room when Maeve found me.

'So you know Gaga's coming back today?' she said.

I nodded. Every guest made extra work for servants, so we always knew when someone was expected.

'I don't know if she's stopping at Ardeevin first,' she said. 'Or coming straight here from her cousin's house.'

At first I wasn't sure why that mattered, and then I remembered Maeve's row with Miss Clayton. Compared to a huge war with guns and bombs, a row with a governess seemed like a very small thing. But that

wasn't fair. The row was important to Maeve, and because of it she might be sent away from her home and her grandmother and all the things that made her feel safe in the world.

Maeve sat down on the bed, messing it up where I'd had it all nice and smooth. Then she saw my face. 'Sorry,' she said, as she jumped up and fixed what she'd done.

'Try not to worry, Maeve,' I said. 'Surely Miss Clayton will have calmed down by now.'

'Not likely,' said Maeve. 'You don't know what she's like. I could be in a lot of trouble when Gaga gets here – if Miss Clayton has told on me …'

'How will you know?' I asked.

'I'll know the second Gaga steps out of the motor car. Her face will tell me – and if she's wearing her angry one, my days in Sligo could very well be numbered.'

'Oh, Maeve!'

'Anyway, nothing I can do about that now,' she

said brightly. 'Why don't you and I go out for a little while?'

Going out with Maeve seemed so tempting, but nowadays that worried me. What if my reference said I was always running off around the estate with her, instead of staying inside doing the work I was paid for?

But in a way, even though Maeve was my friend, she was also my boss. Didn't that mean I had to do what she asked?

'I'll fix it with Mrs Bailey,' she said. 'I'll tell her the whole thing was my idea, and you didn't have any choice in the matter at all!'

'I'm not sure,' I said. 'I love spending time with you, but I feel guilty about Nellie. You and I are always going off together these days, and she never complains, but even so …'

'Well then, Nellie can come too.'

And simply as that, it was decided.

* * *

Ten minutes later, the three of us had our coats on, and were standing in the porte cochère – a place Nellie and I weren't usually allowed, unless it needed cleaning.

'Will we go round to the stables?' said Maeve. 'I know you've only got half an hour, so there won't be time to ride Star, but we could bring some treats, and pet her.'

'We can do whatever you like, Miss Maeve,' said Nellie politely.

But I wasn't ready to go anywhere near the stables. I wasn't ready to see Sam. I wasn't ready to watch him, all excited as he did a very stupid thing.

'No,' I said. 'Let's go to the beach and throw pebbles into the waves. Is that all right with you both? We can close our eyes and make wishes, and maybe they'll come true.'

So the three of us began to walk. Maeve put her

arm around me, and I held Nellie's hand, as all the wishes I wanted to make raced around my head, making me feel dizzy and sick.

* * *

After we'd made our wishes and thrown our pebbles, I began to collect shells, shaking sand off them, and slipping them into my coat pocket.

'What do you want those for?' asked Maeve. 'They're just boring old shells.'

'I bring them home to Winnie and Anne. They have a big collection.'

'I remember,' said Nellie. 'I saw them all lined up outside your house.'

Maeve stared at me for a minute. 'Winnie and Anne are so lucky. I wish I had a big sister like you.'

I was pleased and embarrassed and didn't know what to say, so I whispered 'thank you', and went back to my search.

'Nellie and I can help,' said Maeve, so I showed them the shells my sisters liked the most.

'This is fun,' said Maeve after a while. 'Let's come collecting every single day. Soon your sisters will have the biggest shell collection in the whole world.'

The three of us chatted and laughed as we began our search. It was nice being on the beach with my two friends. Maeve never did things by halves. While Nellie spent ages picking up shells and discarding them if they weren't whole and perfect, Maeve picked up every single one she saw, and stuffed them into the pockets of her fine coat. When her pockets were full, she made a big pile of shells on the sand.

'Oh, no,' I said suddenly. 'What time is it?'

Maeve pulled up her sleeve and looked at her wristwatch (which I loved so very much, and she barely seemed to notice).

'Half past twelve.'

'Nellie and I have to go,' I said.

Maeve held up the hem of her dress, and tried to

gather up all the shells.

'Come on Nellie,' she said. 'You'll have to help carry some of these.'

'Stop!' I said, laughing. 'I won't be able to bring all these on the bicycle when I'm going home – and anyway, my Daddy always said when you're collecting things it's best to leave some for the next person who comes along.'

Reluctantly Maeve dropped the shells, then we held hands as we ran back towards the house.

'Listen? Do you hear?' Maeve stopped running, as we came close.

'What?' I asked. 'Is Mrs Bailey calling us? Does she sound very cross?'

'We should have been back ages ago,' said Nellie, looking terrified.

'No, it's not Mrs Bailey. It's a motor car,' said Maeve.

She was right. Now I could hear the low grumble of the engine too.

'Gaga!' said Maeve. 'I think Gaga is back. Come

on, girls. I have to look at her face and see how much trouble I'm in.'

We went through the kitchen entrance, and immediately bumped into Mrs Bailey.

'Nice to see you, Lily and Nellie,' she said in a sarcastic voice. 'Are you ready to do some work?'

Before I could answer, Maeve stepped between us. 'I'm so sorry Lily and Nellie are a teensy bit late, Mrs Bailey,' she said. 'It's all my fault. I know they have work to do, but I'm afraid I need them to help me with something important upstairs first.'

Now poor Nellie looked even more scared than before. 'I can stay here and get started on the jobs if you like, Mrs Bailey,' she said.

'That seems like a good idea,' said Mrs Bailey. 'Off you go with Maeve, Lily, and be back as quick as you can.'

'Yes, Mrs Bailey,' I said. Then I didn't resist as Maeve dragged me up the servants' stairs, and across the hall, where we could peep out the window, to the

porte cochère.

'Phew, we're just in time,' said Maeve, as the beautiful dark blue Wolseley motor car pulled up outside. We watched as Albert the driver got out, straightened his cap, and then went to open the door for Gaga.

As usual, Gaga was beautifully dressed, wearing a long green wool coat with a fur collar, and a matching hat made of rich velvet. On her face she was wearing the angriest expression I'd ever seen.

'Miss Clayton told her!' said Maeve. 'Gaga knows what I did, and I am doomed.'

'I think we're both doomed if I'm caught here!' I said nervously, as Gaga came up the steps towards the front door.

'Quick, hide,' said Maeve, dragging me behind some huge plants in the corner of the hall.

I hardly dared to breathe as the front door opened and Gaga marched in. If she saw us hiding like criminals, I could forget about a good reference.

'Lady Gore-Booth, so nice to see you back at Lissadell.' Mr Kilgallon had appeared and was standing right next to us. I wondered why he couldn't hear the terrible loud thumping of my heart.

'Can I get you some tea, my lady?' asked the butler.

'Thank you, but no, Kilgallon,' she said. 'I urgently need to talk to Lady Mary. Do you know where she is?'

'In her study, my lady,' he said, giving a little bow, which made the leaves of the plant rustle in a very scary way. 'Please ring if you need anything.'

Then he went back downstairs, and Gaga hurried along to Lady Mary's study.

'Let's go,' said Maeve as soon as the hallway was quiet.

'Where?' I asked, though in my heart I already knew.

Instead of answering, Maeve tiptoed along the corridor towards Lady Mary's study. Halfway there she turned back to me. 'Come on, Lily,' she said. 'But

be as quiet as you can.'

It was easy for her to tiptoe in her dainty shoes, but in my clumpy boots it was a bit harder. I thought about taking them off, but Maeve was beckoning me impatiently, and undoing the thick laces would take me ages. (And besides, I was fairly sure there was a huge hole in the toe of one of my stockings.) So, I sort of slid my feet along the shiny floor, and followed Maeve until we were outside the study. The door was slightly open, which seemed to make Maeve happy, but filled me with dread. From inside, I could hear the sound of Gaga's voice.

'… and poor Miss Clayton has the patience of a saint, but I have never seen her so upset. I had to promise to buy her a new skirt, and new shoes too, though they were barely marked at all.'

'And was Miss Clayton happy then?' asked Lady Mary.

'Oh, not really, but she'll get over it – she's had lots of practice, after all.'

'So everything is all right?'

'It's all right for the moment – but where Maeve is concerned, there's always another spat lurking around the corner. Oh, Mary, you know I love that dear child with all my heart, but she's running wild around the countryside, and it's not right. That servant girl she's always with, Lizzie or Libby or something, I think her name is – she must be a bad influence.'

What?

Gaga was blaming *me*?

That was so unfair!

I wanted to march right in there with my big clumpy boots and tell her exactly what I thought of her opinion. But how could I do that? I'd probably make no difference and lose my job anyway. I was angry and sad at the same time, and I could feel tears beginning to sting my eyes.

Maeve tapped my shoulder and shook her head, showing she didn't agree with her grandmother's words.

Then I could hear Lady Mary's lovely gentle voice. 'I think you must mean Lily,' she said.

I held my breath. Was she going to blame me too? Lady Mary had always been so kind, giving me presents, and fabric to make clothes for Mam and my sisters. All of a sudden, I wanted to walk away. I didn't care anymore if anyone heard me. I wanted to be back downstairs with Nellie and the other servants – back where I belonged.

But Maeve held my arm tightly, and she was my friend, and she was upset, and so I stayed.

'Yes, Lily, that's the girl I mean,' said Gaga.

And then Lady Mary spoke again. 'Well, in that case I'm afraid you're mistaken. Lily is a good, responsible girl, who has never given the slightest trouble. If someone is a bad influence, then I doubt very much if Lily is the culprit.'

When I heard those words, all my anger faded away. I still wanted to march into the room, but now it was to hug Lady Mary. She was a good woman,

and I shouldn't have doubted her.

'Oh, Mary,' said Gaga then. 'You are right of course. I know how strong-willed Maeve is – she's far too like her mother in that respect.'

At these words, Maeve smiled. She loved when people said she was like her mother, even if it was meant in a bad way.

'So what do you plan to do?' asked Lady Mary.

There was a long silence, during which Maeve squeezed my arm so tightly, I was sure she'd leave the print of her fingers on my skin.

'Maeve is a young lady,' said Gaga. 'And she has to start behaving like one. A good, strict boarding school in England is the best place for her. Parting with her will break my heart, but it has to be done.'

'And will her mother agree?' asked Lady Mary.

'I will write to her tomorrow, and once she hears what has been happening, she will understand there isn't any choice. Now, I think I need to lie down for a while. This excitement is all too much for me.'

There was the scraping of chairs, and Maeve and I ran as fast as we could to the top of the servants' stairs, pulling the door closed behind us.

It was dark, but as I hugged Maeve, I could feel her shoulders shaking. Soon she was sobbing so loudly, I was afraid we'd surely be discovered.

'Hush,' I said, soothing her like a baby. 'Hush now, Maeve. It will be fine, I'm sure.'

But I wasn't sure at all. Maeve was rich, but she wasn't a grown-up, and at times like this, grown-ups had all the power. Maeve's life was going to change, and there was nothing we could do about it.

Maeve spent the rest of the day lying on her bed. Whenever I got a chance, I made an excuse to go to her, but there was nothing I could do. She wouldn't look at me. She wouldn't talk to me. She just lay there and cried and cried as if her heart was going to break.

Chapter Seven

That evening, as I walked along the servants' corridor, a figure jumped out of the shadows, and pulled me into the china room, closing the door behind us. I was frightened at first, but when I saw Sam, the fear slipped away, and a kind of emptiness took its place. Everything was changing. Maeve was going to leave Lissadell. Sam was going to leave Lissadell. Maybe neither of them would ever come back again. Maybe I was never going to leave. Maybe I'd be stuck there forever, watching as my friends moved on without me.

'Please don't be cross with me, Lily,' said Sam. 'Don't make me sorry I told you my plans.'

Was I sorry he'd told me? I really wasn't sure. If Sam hadn't told me about signing up, I'd have woken up one day to find him gone. But now that I knew, I

had a decision to make – one of the hardest decisions of my life.

Suddenly I had an idea. Sam wanted adventure and excitement, but he hadn't thought about what war was really like. 'Don't go anywhere,' I said. 'I'll be right back.'

I ran upstairs to the drawing room, which luckily was empty except for a huge hairy dog who was twitching his paws and snoring loudly. I scanned the headlines of the newspapers on the table, grabbed one, and ran back down to Sam.

'Here,' I said, holding the paper towards him. 'Read this, and see what you think. Read about the dirt and the trenches and the fear. Read about all our fine young men who have died.'

He shook his head. 'I'm not reading it. I'm not changing my mind.'

Now I was angry, but not just at him. I was angry at Miss Clayton. I was angry at Gaga. I was angry at the recruiting soldiers who didn't care how old Sam

was. I was angry at Miss O'Brien who wouldn't make her mind up to get married. I was angry at the whole world.

'How can you go off to fight if you're afraid of a stupid newspaper?' I shouted. 'Paper and ink can't hurt you, but bombs and bullets can.' I shoved the paper right into his face, making him back into a corner. 'Read it!' I said. 'Please read it, Sam.'

His voice was so low, I couldn't make out his words.

'What did you say?' I asked.

'I can't read, Lily. I don't know how.'

'Oh, Sam!' I said, dropping the newspaper to the floor. 'I'm so sorry. I shouldn't have …'

'Don't be sorry,' he said. 'It's all my own fault. For years I skipped off school any chance I got. Martin and I spent more time running around the fields than at our desks. We had good fun, the two of us, though I know now we weren't being very clever.'

'I can teach you!' I said. 'Nellie couldn't read before, but after lessons with me she can read anything at

all – even the big, long words in the newspapers. In a few weeks you'll be …'

'In a few weeks I'll be far away from here. Thank you for your offer, Lily, but it's too late.'

'But …' I didn't finish. I'm good at arguing (too good sometimes, according to Mam), but I didn't know any words that would make him change his mind. I put my hand on the door handle, and noticed that my fingers were covered with dark black ink. It used to be Harry's job to iron the newspapers and stop the ink from staining things, but because of the stupid war, Harry wasn't back at Lissadell yet. Because of the stupid war, Sam was going to leave, and maybe he …

'Wait,' said Sam, as he took a small package from his pocket and handed it to me. It was something hard and lumpy, all wrapped up in old newspaper and tied with string.

'For me?' I asked.

'Yes – well really it's for your brothers. I made a lion

and a bear, because that's what you said they liked.'

Suddenly I remembered the gloves, which were still in my apron pocket.

'These are for you, from my Mam,' I said as I handed them to him. 'To thank you for making the animals for the children.'

'Are they really for me?' he asked as he pulled off the brown paper. 'No one ever gives me presents.'

And he looked so shy, and so grateful and so young, I thought my heart was going to break.

'They are perfect,' he said when he put the gloves on. 'Tell your mam I love them. Tell her they'll keep my hands lovely and warm when I'm in ...'

I didn't wait to hear the rest. I opened the door and ran quickly away from him.

* * *

'Look, Lily,' said Nellie patiently, holding her knitting towards me. 'Turning the heel is easy. Just watch

what I do, and you'll see. You pick up this stitch here, and put in on the other needle. Then you ...'

Usually I could turn a heel without even thinking about it, but tonight my mind was somewhere else. I tried to do what Nellie said, but I dropped the stitch, and when I was picking it up, I dropped three more, making a big hole. Suddenly I didn't care if I dropped every single stitch. I was tired of knitting. I was tired of everything.

'Lily,' said Nellie, putting down her knitting and coming to sit next to me on my bed. 'What is it? What's wrong with you tonight? Are you worried about the war again? Maybe it will be over soon. I heard Mr Kilgallon say that our boys had a big victory yesterday.'

She was smiling at me, and her big blue eyes were so gentle and kind. I really, really wanted to tell her about Sam, but I'd promised him – and I hated to break my promise – so instead I told her about Maeve.

'Poor Maeve,' said Nellie when I'd finished. 'No

wonder she's so upset. I'd hate to be sent back to school.'

Nellie didn't have happy memories of school the way I did. The teacher in the workhouse had been very cross and mean, hitting the children with a big stick when they didn't understand things.

'So what happens next?' she asked.

'Maeve has to wait for Gaga's letter to get to the Countess – and for the reply to come back here.'

'That won't take long, will it?'

'Who knows? And when the letter gets to Dublin, The Countess might not even be there,' I said, remembering all the stories I'd read in the papers about Maeve's mother. 'She could be off leading a revolution or something.'

'So Maeve will have to be patient.'

I smiled at her. 'And I'm afraid Maeve isn't at all like you – she's not a very patient person.'

I felt so sorry for Maeve. Waiting is the hardest thing of all, I thought.

'What do you think Maeve's mother will say? Will she agree with Gaga?' asked Nellie.

'Who knows? The Countess never seems to do what people expect. Only thing is, she's trusted Gaga to take care of Maeve for all these years, so I suppose she'll go along with her in this too. I'm afraid Maeve might be sent away very, very soon.'

Nellie put her arm around me. 'Poor Maeve,' she said. 'And poor you.'

Chapter Eight

'**A**h, there you are, Lily,' said Lady Mary next morning as I carried my mop and bucket into the front hall. 'We've been looking for you. Can you go downstairs and change out of your uniform, and get your coat, please? We're going on a journey, and Albert will be here soon with the motor car.'

Maeve was standing next to Lady Mary, carrying a large basket, which was covered with one of Cook's best red and white checked cloths.

I rubbed my eyes. I hadn't slept well the night before and now I was confused.

Why was Maeve smiling so brightly?

Had the decision about her school been made already?

Why was *I* going with her?

Did girls in boarding schools have maids?

Did I want to go to England?

It sounded like fun, but what about my family, what about my hopes of being a teacher?

'But ...'

'Don't worry about your work, Lily,' said Lady Mary. 'I've already had a word with Mrs Bailey.'

Outside I heard the beep of the motor car horn, so I knew there was no time for questions. In my room, I changed into my Sunday dress and grabbed my coat and gloves. Then I hurried back upstairs, wondering what the day was going to hold.

* * *

Soon I was sitting in the back of the motor car, with Lady Mary on one side of me and Maeve on the other. I'd been in the motor car a few times before, but it was still exciting – much more exciting than a day of work.

'You must be wondering what all this is about,

Lily?' said Lady Mary as we drove out through the big gates.

I nodded. Of course I was wondering about lots of things.

Why exactly were we making this journey?

Why did Lady Mary have a bundle of sheets and towels on her knee?

'We're going to Sligo Town,' said Lady Mary. I got word last night that there's a new family of refugees coming from Belgium today, so I want to go and arrange a house for them.'

I smiled. This was very good news. I was glad Maeve wasn't going away to school today, and welcoming refugees was a nice job. (Well, nice for us, anyway. *They* probably wished they were at home in their own houses, doing whatever things they usually do on a normal Wednesday morning.) I remembered the last refugees we had welcomed – a mam, a dad and four very sweet children. I'd played games with the little ones, and taught them some words in English, and

after seeing that, Lady Mary asked me to give lessons to her own little boys, Michael and Hugh.

'You are very kind, Lady Mary,' I said.

'It's the least I can do for these poor people,' she replied. 'And after yesterday, when Maeve ... well Maeve had a difficult day, so I thought it would be nice for her to come along too.'

'And I suggested that you could come, Lily,' said Maeve. 'We can all help to make the house nice for the new family.'

I looked at Maeve, and once again, I couldn't understand why she seemed so happy. Yesterday, she'd wailed and cried so much I thought her bedroom would be flooded with tears, and now she looked as if she didn't have a care in the world. Going to Sligo Town was a nice treat, but was it enough to make her forget about the threat of going to boarding school?

Then Maeve started to sing, and Albert joined in, and Lady Mary hummed along as she wrote lists in her notebook, and I decided that for a little while I

wasn't going to worry about anything. I was going to sing along, and enjoy the journey.

* * *

First we went to visit the Belgian family I had met before. The woman opened the door, and I was delighted when she remembered me. 'Lily!' she said, reaching out to shake my hand. 'Lovely Lily.'

The baby in her arms reached for me, and when I took her, I was so happy at how plump and healthy she'd become. Now her eyes were shining, and she gurgled happily as she played with my hair.

We all followed the woman inside, where the three older children ran to me in delight. They seemed taller and stronger and brighter than the grubby little scraps I'd taught a few words of English to on my last visit. I set the baby on the rug, and picked up the toy cat I'd used before. 'Do you remember?' I said to the older children in a slow, clear voice. 'This is a cat.'

The little girls laughed as the older boy took the cat from me. 'I know is a cat,' he said. 'I know very much of English now. Not like before. Papa is at work.'

'Pretty dress,' said one of his sisters, patting my skirt.

'Come and have nice cake,' said the other girl, taking my hand and pulling me to the table. 'Mama make nice cake for you.'

So we all sat at the table. I held the baby, while the next littlest girl sat on Maeve's knee, and played with her gold bracelet. We drank a strange but delicious hot drink, and ate sweet cake, and the children played and laughed and we had a very pleasant hour.

'That's a good thing you have done, Lady Mary,' I said as the Belgian woman left the table to deal with a squabble between her two oldest children. 'These people must miss their homes, but I can see they are warm and comfortable, and as happy as it is possible to be in a country that is strange to them.'

'You helped too, Lily,' she said. 'And many others

also – and when everyone helps, it's easy to make a difference. Now it's time for us to go – we have another new family to welcome.'

* * *

Albert followed the directions Lady Mary gave him, and soon he stopped the motor car outside a small little cottage at the edge of the town. As we climbed out and stretched, the door opened and a familiar woman stepped outside.

'Sadie!' said Lady Mary. 'So nice to see you again.'

Sadie was the local priest's housekeeper, and she did lots of work settling refugee families into their new homes.

'Nice to see you too, Lady Mary,' she said. 'But I think you've had a wasted journey. It's a small family this time – just a mam and dad and their two boys. They are all settled in, and have everything they need.'

'I'm happy to hear it,' said Lady Mary. 'Why don't

we go in and say hello, and then I can go on to my meeting?'

'As you wish,' said Sadie. 'I won't delay – I promised Father Murphy I'd have a nice fruitcake ready for his afternoon tea.'

Sadie went off in the direction of the town, and the rest of us walked towards the cottage. 'You'll like this,' I said to Maeve. 'It's so nice teaching the Belgian children their first English words.'

Lady Mary lifted her hand, but before she could knock, the door opened and a man and woman stepped outside. They didn't look very pleased to see us.

'Hello,' said Lady Mary, in a slow, loud voice, pointing at herself, and then them. 'We – help – you? You – need – things?'

The woman scratched her head, and the man glared at us. They didn't seem to understand that this was a real Lady, and that they should be polite to her, and honoured that she was on their doorstep.

'We need no things,' he said in a deep voice with a strange accent. 'Other lady give us many things. You go now.'

I felt embarrassed for Lady Mary, who was trying to be nice, and wasn't used to being spoken to like that.

'What about the children?' I asked. 'Can we see them?'

The man didn't answer, but he looked over his shoulder and shouted something through the open door. From inside, a voice shouted back, and a second later, two boys stepped out into the sunlight. They were about twelve or thirteen years old. I took a small step backwards as they stood next to their parents. I didn't mind that they were dirty, and their hair was uncombed, and their clothes were old and patched. I *did* mind that they were staring at us in a very scary way. There had been plenty of rough boys in my old school, but none as rough as these two. There was no way I was going to sit down and teach English to

these boys – I'd have been much too frightened.

Lady Mary had gone pale, but still, she smiled at the family. She held out the bundle of sheets and towels. The woman took them and tossed them through the door, where they fell on the bare stone floor. She didn't say thank you in English, or any other language. She didn't say anything at all. I wanted to go in and grab the linen back – the sheets were so much nicer than the ones Mam had for our beds. The towels were softer than any she could even dream of owning.

'*Hey,*' I wanted to say to the Belgians. '*That's the Gore-Booth's best linen. You should treat it with respect. You should treat us with respect. We're doing our best to help you.*'

But I was too afraid of the rough boys to say anything at all.

'Well then,' said Lady Mary, with a weak smile. 'It was very nice to meet you, but we'd best be off. Just let Sadie know if you need anything else, and I'll

make sure it's provided. Now come along, girls.'

The man spat on the ground near us, just missing the toe of Lady Mary's fine left boot. Then the family went back inside the cottage, slamming the door behind them.

'Well, that wasn't very nice,' I said. 'Why couldn't they be more grateful?'

Lady Mary smiled at me. 'I agree that wasn't very pleasant, Lily,' she said. 'But we must try to be understanding.'

'But they were so *rude*,' I said.

'Indeed they were,' she said. 'But they have been through a terrible time. They have lost their homes and most of their belongings. They may have lost family and friends. We can only guess at the horrors they have seen.'

Now I felt bad. Suddenly, as I looked at Lady Mary, standing on the dusty street in her fine clothes, with her hair all pinned and curled, she reminded me of my mam. Of course, Mam didn't look anything like

Lady Mary. Mam dressed in faded clothes that were soft from years of washing. She was wrinkled and worn from endless hard work – but both women were gentle and kind. Both women were ready to see the best in everyone, even people who didn't seem to deserve it.

'You're right, Lady Mary. I'm sorry.'

'Thank you,' she said. 'What do you think about all of this, Maeve?'

I'd been so distracted by the Belgian family, I hadn't paid much attention to Maeve. Now I looked at her properly. She didn't reply to her aunt. She had a half-smile on her face as if, in her head, she was somewhere else completely.

'Maeve?' I said. 'Are you all right?' Now I noticed that she was still carrying the basket I'd seen earlier. 'Is that food for the Belgians? Did you forget to give it to them? I know they weren't very nice, but I agree with Lady Mary. Maybe we should make allowances, because of all they've been through. I'll wait with

you, and protect you, if you want to knock on the door and give it to them.'

This was brave of me, as no matter what Lady Mary said, I was still a bit afraid of those two rough-looking boys.

'Oh,' said Maeve, dreamily. 'Thank you, Lily, but the basket isn't for the Belgians – it's for us.'

I didn't understand, but now Lady Mary spoke again. 'I may as well move on to my meeting. I'm planning a concert to raise money for the war effort, and I have arranged to talk to some people who have done something similar. What are you two girls going to do?'

I didn't have a plan. I'd thought I'd be spending the day with cute little Belgian babies, playing with them and teaching them English.

'Oh, don't worry about us, Aunt Mary,' said Maeve. 'Lily and I are used to entertaining ourselves, and we've both been to Sligo Town before, so we won't get lost or anything.'

'Very well. I will meet you in the square at four o'clock.' Lady Mary opened her pretty beaded purse and took out some money, which she handed to Maeve. 'Go to the hotel and buy yourself some lunch. Have a nice time, and I will see you later.'

I watched as she hurried away. I loved that woman so much. I wondered if Maeve wished Lady Mary was her mam, instead of her own exciting, unpredictable, hard-to-pin-down mother. Did she wish for a mam who was calm and kind and gentle and always there?

But then I knew the answer. You have to love the mam you've got, because she's all you know – that's the way the world works. And even if she's not perfect, she's your mam, and is special to you.

Chapter Nine

'What do you want to do, Maeve?' I asked, as the dust raised by Lady Mary's footsteps vanished in the breeze. 'Are you hungry? Is it too early for lunch? Don't forget I've been up since six o'clock, and my breakfast is only a distant memory. We could ...'

'Oh, Lily,' she said. 'I have the best surprise for you.'

'I like the sound of that. Are we going to a fancy hotel for lunch as Lady Mary said?'

'No.'

'Are we going for a walk along the river? When Mam and Dad were courting they did that. She said the river is called the Garavogue and I think that's such a lovely romantic name. Is that where we're going?'

'No.' She smiled as she shook her head. I don't

know if I'd ever seen her so happy, which was strange, when she'd been crying her eyes out only the night before. 'If I tell you, it won't be a surprise, will it? Now come along with me, or we'll be late.'

I wondered what we were going to be late for, but I didn't ask any more questions. Maeve seemed to know where she was going, and she was in a happy mood, so we chatted and laughed as we strolled along. As usual when I was with Maeve, I had a lovely sense of excitement, a sense that I'd no idea what was going to happen next, a sense that adventure was waiting for us just around the corner.

* * *

'Oh, stop, Maeve! I know this street. I know this shop.'

I stared through the little shop window at the gorgeous display of handkerchiefs and gloves. 'This shop belongs to ...'

'Lily!' I was nearly knocked to the ground, as a girl ran at me in a whirlwind of laughter and long hair and skirts and ribbons.

'Rose!' We hugged for a long time, and when we untangled ourselves, I turned to Maeve. 'Maeve, this is Rose,' I said.

Maeve held out her hand politely. 'Hello, Rose. You're Lily's friend from school. She often talks about you and Hanora. It sounds as if you three had a lot of fun together.'

'Pleased to meet you, Maeve,' said Rose as they shook hands. She didn't say anything else, but I knew she had to be wondering why I was strolling around Sligo town with a rich girl like this. I'd never told Hanora and Rose about my friendship with Maeve, fearing they wouldn't understand. Now that I saw my two friends together though, I was sorry. They were just two young Irish girls with their own hopes and dreams and wishes.

'I got a letter from Hanora last week,' I said. 'She

sounds very happy. I wonder if she'll ever come back from America.'

'Would *you* come back?' laughed Rose. 'It sounds like a wonderful place, not like boring old Sligo.'

'I'd love to visit America,' sighed Maeve.

So the three of us chatted for a while, and it was lovely.

'Have you time to spare?' asked Rose then. 'I could ask my aunt for a half hour off, and the three of us could go and get a cup of tea together. I know a lovely little tea-house, and it won't be busy at this time.'

That sounded like a good idea to me, but when I looked at Maeve, she checked her lovely wristwatch and shook her head.

'I'm sorry, Rose,' she said. 'It would be very nice, but if we don't go now … we'll miss … well, if you don't mind, we have to go right away. Lily and I are going on an adventure.'

'That sounds exciting,' said Rose. 'Where are you going?'

'I wish I knew!' I said. 'It's a surprise, and Maeve won't tell me what it is.'

'I can tell *you*, Rose,' said Maeve, and when Rose nodded happily, Maeve leaned closer and whispered in her ear.

Rose's eyes went wide. 'You lucky, lucky girl, Lily,' she said. 'And stop hanging around here – you definitely don't want to be late for this surprise.'

Now I was excited all over again, and it was a great feeling – all buzzy and warm. We hugged, and said our goodbyes, and then Maeve picked up her basket and the two of us set off down the street. After a few steps, Maeve stopped walking and we both turned back to where Rose was still standing outside her uncle and aunt's shop, waving.

'Sorry we couldn't stay for tea,' called Maeve. 'Next time I'll treat the three of us to a huge plate of the finest cream buns in Sligo.'

And because it was Maeve, I know it would very likely happen – if only she wasn't far away in England

at boarding school.

* * *

I couldn't imagine why Rose thought Sligo Town was boring. There was so much to see – with lots of people on the footpaths, and ponies and carts and even an occasional motor car. Even though I'd been there before, I was soon completely lost, but Maeve walked confidently, never hesitating for a second.

'Can you tell me what the surprise is yet?' I asked after a while.

'Almost there,' said Maeve.

We turned a corner, and all of a sudden, I knew where we were.

'The railway station?' I said. 'Is that the surprise?'

I'd been to the railway station with Lady Mary, when we went to meet the first family of Belgian refugees. Now I thought I understood.

'Is there another refugee family coming? Maybe

this one will have sweet little children we can play with? But why didn't Lady Mary come with us? Is she trusting us to know what to do and what to say?'

Maeve laughed. 'You're wrong, Lily. That's not the surprise. We're not meeting another refugee family. In fact, we're not meeting anyone at all.'

'So we're not actually going to the railway station? Is there something else along this street?' I couldn't see anything interesting up ahead, but didn't say so. Maeve had arranged a surprise and I didn't want to sound ungrateful.

Maeve laughed again, and I could see she was delighted with all my questions. 'Oh we *are* going to the railway station,' she said. 'But we're not meeting any travellers.'

'Then why?'

'We *are* the travellers.'

It took a second for me to understand, and when I did, the words came rushing out. 'You mean we're going on a journey? On a train? Oh, Maeve, can it

really be true?'

'Yes, Lily. It's really true.'

I'd never been on a train before. They seemed big and noisy and so very exciting. I hadn't even stepped aboard, and already I was looking forward to telling my little brothers about it. I was already picturing their shining eyes, and imagining all the questions they'd ask, rushing out the words, competing to see who could find out the most, already planning what they'd tell their friends at school.

Maeve checked her wristwatch again – (I was too excited to be jealous of it this time!) 'If we're going on the train, we'd better get a move on – it leaves in ten minutes.'

We were walking quickly now and were already at the door of the station. Maeve led the way inside, with no hesitation, with her head held high, as if she went on train journeys every day of her life.

I followed as she went towards the ticket office. I was so excited I could hardly think straight. I won-

dered where we were going. Could it be Collooney, or maybe even all the way to Ballymote, which was much further than I'd ever, ever been, further than my mam or daddy had ever travelled in their whole lives.

A customer stepped away from the ticket office window, tucking his ticket carefully into the pocket of his jacket. Maeve stepped forward, right up to the glass screen.

'What can I do for you, young lady?' asked the man.

'We'd like two train tickets, please,' said Maeve.

'Then you've come to the right place,' he said. 'Where would you like to go?'

'We'd like to go to Dublin,' said Maeve, and as she took money from her purse, I thought I was going to faint away from the excitement of it all.

Chapter Ten

'Are you happy, Lily?' asked Maeve, when we were on the train and settled into two window seats facing each other. 'Isn't this a good surprise? Is this the best surprise you've ever had?'

I was in shock, and my mouth didn't seem able to form any words.

'It's ... so ... I'm ...'

I stopped muttering as the loudest whistle I'd ever heard shrieked in the distance. There was the sound of doors slamming, and slowly the train began to move. I saw the ticket man pull down a blind, as if he were shutting up and going away for his dinner. On the platform, a man with a whistle and a big red flag was walking away towards an open door-way. A woman with a crying baby ran along beside us, waving like mad at someone I couldn't see. Some

crows paid no attention at all to the noise of the train, as they fought over a discarded crust. Further along the carriage, two men put suitcases on a metal rack over their heads, and then settled in their seats and unfolded their newspapers.

I was going to Dublin!

I, Lily Brennan from Sligo was on a train with my friend, and we were going to Dublin.

How could this even be true?

* * *

The train had picked up speed, and I was enjoying the chugga-chug sound of the wheels, and the sway of the carriage as we quickly left the town, and travelled through the countryside. Some children stood on a gate and waved at us, and by the time I thought to wave back at them they were already far away.

Maeve took off her coat and lay it neatly on the seat beside her.

'You probably have a few questions for me,' she said.

A *few* questions? I had so many, I hardly knew where to start. So I said nothing, waiting for her to continue.

'We're going to visit Mother,' she said. 'That's the real surprise. I know you like seeing her, and she likes seeing you, so the three of us will have a lovely time together I'm sure.'

'Yes, I'm sure we will,' I said weakly, trying not to think what Mam would say when she heard about this – her own girl going on a train to Dublin to spend time with a real, live countess.

'But Dublin is so far away,' I continued. I didn't know exactly how far it was, but I knew it was miles and miles and miles. 'Will we be back at Lissadell in time for bed?'

'That's another surprise – we're not going back to Lissadell tonight – we're going to stay with Mother in her house in Dublin.'

This was both exciting and scary. 'But I didn't bring my hairbrush, or clean stockings or anything else. A surprise is nice, but if you'd told me ...'

'Oh, don't worry about that. Mother will lend us anything we need.'

I tried hard, but couldn't imagine a world where I'd be borrowing things from the countess. 'How long are we staying?' I asked. 'One night? Or two?' Did I dare say it? 'More than that?'

Maeve shrugged. 'Oh, I'm not sure yet how long we'll stay. Let's just see how we get on. That's what you do when you're on an adventure.'

Any adventures I'd had with Nellie, or Rose and Hanora usually involved a walk by the sea or a river, or across the hilly fields behind the church. I didn't know how to imagine an adventure that involved a train journey – all the way to Dublin!

'And Mrs Bailey doesn't mind me being away from my work? I don't think there are any new guests expected over the next few days, but she always finds

plenty for me to do.'

'Oh, you know what Mrs Bailey is like,' said Maeve. 'She might mutter a bit, but as long as you're with me she won't mind at all. I'm sure she's happy for you to be having such an exciting time.'

I wasn't sure about that at all.

'And Lady Mary and Sir Josslyn and your grand-mother? Are they really happy about you going to Dublin?'

'They know I miss Mother and don't see her enough.'

And then I thought I understood. Gaga had already made up her mind about Maeve going to school, and she was allowing this trip, so Maeve and her mother could meet one more time before Maeve was sent away. Did Maeve understand this, though? If she did, why was she so happy? Was the thought of seeing her mother for a few days going to make up for months and years at school far away in England?

I didn't ask Maeve any of this, though. I wanted her

happy mood to last, and I was afraid of her answers. So instead I asked an easier question.

'Didn't Lady Mary and Gaga mind you going to Dublin without another adult, with just me?'

'What do we need adults for? We're not babies, and I've been to Dublin on a train before, you know.'

'You have?'

'Yes – lots of times, before you came to Lissadell. Gaga used bring me to the Horse Show every August, and it was so much fun. Sometimes Mother met us and we'd go for lunch in a very fancy restaurant.'

'So you know what to do?'

'About what?'

'Well, where do we get off the train? How do we know when we're in Dublin? How do we open the door? What if we can't get off on time – and the train goes on to the next stop?'

'We'll know it's Dublin because we'll see all the huge, big houses – and anyway, there will be a sign on the wall of the station. And we will have plenty of

time to get off, because it's the last stop. Now don't worry any more, Lily. Sit back and enjoy the journey.'

I tried to do what she said. I took off my coat and folded it the way Maeve had folded hers, being careful to cover one of the elbows, which had been darned more than once. I arranged my gloves neatly on top of it. Maeve gave me a lemon drop from her purse, and I sucked it, enjoying the sweet-sharp tang on my tongue. I sat back in my seat and looked out the window at a field of sheep. I often complained that my life at Lissadell was boring, and now, here I was, in the middle of the most exciting thing I'd ever done in my whole life. I should have been very happy, and I sort of was – but one thing was bothering me, and it was dancing around the edges of my brain, almost teasing me. We'd gone another few miles, and I'd sucked my lemon drop until it was only the tiniest sliver of sweetness on my tongue, when I knew what was wrong.

'Lady Mary!' I said.

'What about her?'

'When she left us outside the Belgian's house, she asked what we were going to do with our time in Sligo – and then she said she'd meet us in the square at four o'clock. Why would she say that? Surely she knew we wouldn't be back from Dublin in time for that?'

All kinds of scary possibilities raced through my head. Did Lady Mary know I was going with Maeve? Maybe she thought Maeve was going on her own, and I was supposed to be at the square in Sligo Town at four, ready to meet Albert, and get back to Lissadell in time to prepare the family bedrooms and dressing rooms for the night? But would she really let Maeve travel all that way on her own?

'This trip was supposed to be a surprise for you, remember?' said Maeve. 'Don't you think it would spoil the surprise if Aunt Mary let the cat out of the bag? If she said, "Have a nice time in Dublin, and I'll see you in a few days."?'

That seemed to make sense, but still I wasn't sure. 'Is that really the truth?'

Maeve gave me a huge smile. 'Would I lie to you?' she asked.

And I was so relieved, and so excited and happy, I didn't notice that she hadn't answered my question at all.

Chapter Eleven

s the train raced through the countryside, I began to relax. The fields and cottages and grassy country lanes were interesting, but the towns we stopped at were even better. Maeve and I watched people on the train platforms, making up stories about who they were, and where they were going.

'Look at that man in the dark coat,' said Maeve when we stopped in Boyle. 'I bet you anything he's a spy. Look how he's got his head down, as if he's afraid of being recognised.'

I laughed. 'You read too many Sherlock Holmes stories – you see spies and robbers everywhere.'

'Who do you see that's interesting, then?'

'See that girl over there, the pretty, dark-haired one with the huge, big suitcase?'

'Yes.'

'Well she's in love with a dashing actor her parents don't approve of. They want her to marry the boring farmer next door who picks his nose and never washes his hands.'

'She's told her parents she's visiting her cousin for a few days,' continued Maeve. 'But really she's running away to meet the actor in Dublin. That suitcase is full of his romantic love letters.'

'They'll go to the best jewellers in the city, and buy a ring with a diamond the size of a peahen's egg.'

'And they'll catch the boat to England and get married and have five clever daughters and live happily ever after.'

And so the towns slipped by, one after the other. Carrick-on-Shannon, Dromod, Longford, Edgeworthstown. Places I'd heard talk of, and seen on an atlas at school, but I'd never dreamed of visiting. At every station lots of people got on and off, but no one ever came and sat near us. I was glad, as I'd have been too shy to talk to them.

After a while, the rumbling of my tummy seemed almost as loud as the sound of the train's engine. I wondered if there was such a thing as a shop or a café on a train, but didn't say anything. If I was wrong, I knew Maeve wouldn't laugh at me, but I'd have felt foolish all the same. Then, when I thought I was about to faint away from the hunger, Maeve reached under her seat and pulled out the basket, which I'd forgotten about in all the excitement.

'Hungry?' she asked. She pulled back the red and white cloth and revealed all kinds of delicious treats – perfect little sandwiches made with soft white bread, pastries, cakes, chocolate, fruit and sweet little bottles of apple juice. Maeve spread white napkins on the little table in front of us, and we ate like two queens.

I'd been up before dawn as usual, so after the food, I sat back in my seat, closed my eyes, and let the regular movement of the train rock me to sleep. I woke to a loud whistle, and then a shout of, 'Dublin. Last stop. Everyone leave the train please. Last stop here.'

Dublin! I was really in Dublin. I could only see the station platform, and already I was thrilled. Crowds bigger than I'd ever seen before pushed past each other, making more noise than I could have imagined. Women held tight to toddlers' hands, and men struggled with bags and suitcases. Laughing boys darted around, ignoring the worried warning shouts of their parents.

I started to feel afraid, but across from me, Maeve was smiling calmly as she packed up the scraps from our picnic, and that made me relax a small bit. I stood, put on my coat and gloves, and followed her in silence as we got off the train, and made our way out of the station.

'Just give me a minute to get my bearings,' said Maeve, as she put down her basket. 'It's a long time since I was here.'

I nodded, and stood beside her, watching the stream of cars and bicycles and horses and carts. I jumped back from the edge of the footpath as a loud

bell rang, and a tram rolled by, so close I could easily have reached out and touched it with my fingers. I stared at the fancily dressed people, who all seemed to know where they were going, and were hurrying to get there.

'This place is so big and noisy,' I said. 'How will your mother know where to find us?'

'Oh, Mother isn't meeting us here.'

'She's not?' My fear hadn't gone very far away – I think it had been tip-toeing along behind me, and now it was back again, tapping on my shoulder.

'Of course not. Don't you know how busy she is?'

I knew Countess Markievicz was in the newspaper a lot, for attending meetings and demonstrations and things, so I suppose that counted as being busy. I thought of Lady Mary, who never once washed a cup or dusted a dresser or changed a dirty nappy, and still never seemed to have a minute to spare.

'So who's coming to meet us instead? Your mother's driver? Have you met him before? Is he nice, like

Albert?'

'I don't think Mother even has a motor car or a driver.'

'So?'

'We'll make our own way to her house.'

Now the fear jumped right up onto my back, and put its cold fingers on my neck.

'But ... this isn't ... I mean this is, it's Dublin!'

'Oh, don't worry so much, Lily. It's not far – I checked it on a map in Uncle Joss's library. We'll be there in no time.'

I stood at the station door minding the basket, while Maeve went and asked a kind lady for directions. Shortly after that, my friend and I were on the top deck of a tram, trundling along the streets of Dublin. Some of the buildings were so tall I had to bend my neck back to see the top of them. There were monuments and statues that were surely as tall as Benbulben. I sat there with my mouth open, not caring that there was dust in my eyes and the wind

was blowing my hair like mad. Maeve laughed as she held on to her hat.

'Isn't this such fun?' she said.

I nodded, feeling like a sophisticated grown-up and a terrified child, all at the same time.

'Here we are,' said Maeve after a while, reading a sign on a wall. 'This is Rathmines.'

'Rathmines? Aren't we in Dublin anymore?'

'It's still Dublin,' she said. 'But the city is so big it's divided into different districts.'

Maeve was good at explaining things without making me feel stupid. She'd make a good teacher, but rich girls like her weren't expected to have jobs.

'When I lived with Mother and Father,' she said. 'We had a lovely house in Rathgar. But now Mother lives somewhere near here. I've never been to this house, but I know the address from the letters we write to each other.'

Poor Maeve. I missed my mam, even though I saw her every single week, on my day off. Maeve went

months and months without seeing her mother, and her daddy was abroad and she hadn't seen him for years. How could a few letters make up for that?

Maeve reached up and rang a bell as we had watched other passengers do, and when the tram stopped, we ran down the funny curved outside staircase, and on to the street.

Four soldiers in uniform marched by. One of them looked more like a boy than a man. Suddenly I felt guilty. With all the excitement of the journey to Dublin, I'd completely forgotten about Sam.

What if he left for the army before Maeve and I got back from Dublin?

What if he went to war before I had time to wish him well and tell him to be safe?

What if I never saw him again?

'Why do you look so sad, Lily?' asked Maeve. 'Is something wrong?'

I wanted to tell her about Sam, but I had to keep my promise, and besides, Maeve had her own prob-

lems to deal with. 'I'm excited, that's all. Do you know where we go from here?'

We were standing at a crossroads. Every house I could see was tall and elegant, with a lovely garden in the front. I wished Mam was with me, so she could see how nice everything was – and so she could mind me, and tell me not to be afraid, and that everything was going to be all right. Maeve spun around on the heel of her pretty shoe, and then pointed at a sign. 'Leinster Road,' she said. 'This is the street we want. Look out for *Surrey House* – that's where Mother lives.'

We walked slowly along the street, reading the names and numbers on the pillars outside each house. I thought how different this was to my own home village, where you know the houses by saying things like 'the second one after the pump' or 'the one with the blue door, across from the church'.

Lots of people passed by, but no one paid us much attention, as they went about their lives, with no idea

what an exciting day this was for me.

'Here it is!' said Maeve triumphantly. 'We're here at last. This is Mother's house.'

I stood at the gate and looked up at the house. Like most on the street, it was three storeys tall, and joined on to the one next to it. It was many, many times bigger than the cottage I grew up in, but compared to Lissadell House, it was tiny. I couldn't see a basement, and wondered where the servants slept. I wondered where I was going to sleep.

'Come along,' said Maeve, marching up the footpath to the front door. 'Time to say hello to Mother.'

Chapter Twelve

Maeve had to knock on the door three times before we heard the sound of footsteps. I held my breath as the door opened slowly and creakily.

The young girl who stood before us was dressed as a servant – but not one who would have lasted five minutes with Mrs Bailey. Her apron was grubby, she wasn't wearing a cap, and her hair was falling around her face in long, greasy strands. She did not look pleased to see us.

'What do you want?' she asked so rudely, that even Maeve was silent for a second. 'If you're begging, we have nothing for you.'

I hid a smile at the thought of Maeve begging, but she didn't look amused.

'And Madame isn't here,' continued the girl. 'Or anyone else either – for a change. Mr James Con-

nolly and his family only left this morning, and Mr Colbert and Mrs Sheehy-Skeffington and that lot haven't shown up today.'

I knew these names from the newspapers, and wondered how the girl could speak so casually about such famous people. I was *very* glad I wouldn't have to talk to any of them.

I wondered why the countess had gone out when her daughter was due to arrive. On Saturday mornings, when I go home, Mam doesn't even go as far as the neighbour's house, in case she wouldn't be there to welcome me with one of her special hugs.

The girl went to close the door, but Maeve put out her foot, stopping her.

'What is your name?' she asked.

'Susan,' said the girl.

'Susan, I am Miss Maeve de Markievicz – Countess Markievicz's daughter,' she said, in a voice that was even posher than usual. 'I would like to come inside to wait for my mother.'

The girl looked doubtful. 'How do I know you're ...?' But then a beautiful spaniel came running down the stairs and jumped right into Maeve's arms.

'Poppet,' said Maeve, hugging the dog and letting it lick her face. 'You know who I am, don't you?'

Even the sulky girl couldn't argue now. She stepped back and didn't protest as Maeve marched into the hallway, still holding Poppet, who was furiously wagging her tail, and whimpering happily. I followed, stepping onto the stained and dirty tiles. I closed the door behind us, as Susan was already walking away.

'When will my mother be back?' asked Maeve.

Susan half-turned to us. 'I don't know, do I? She doesn't tell me about her comings and goings.'

Maeve put Poppet down, and took off her coat, holding it out, as if waiting for someone to take it from her and hang it up.

'Where is the footman?' she asked.

'There's no footman here,' said Susan.

'Just a butler then?' said Maeve.

Now Susan actually laughed a hoarse laugh that turned into a horrible raspy cough.

'There's no one else here,' she said when the coughing fit was over. 'There's always only me – and I've got to do *everything!*'

By the looks of the house, she didn't do very much, but that wasn't really any of my business.

'Where should we wait?' asked Maeve, as she hung her coat on a stand that already held a collection of coats of all kinds – some made of rich satin and wool, and some ragged old ones that looked as if they belonged to beggars.

Susan shrugged, and then waved vaguely towards a door on our left. 'In there, I suppose. You won't be wanting tea.'

Tea sounded lovely, but Susan wasn't asking the question. She pushed the door open with her foot and then hurried to the end of the hallway, and through a door which she slammed firmly behind her.

Maeve turned to me. 'Welcome to Dublin,' she said.

* * *

The room had big high ceilings, and on the walls there were lots of paintings in fancy frames. The chairs were fancy too, a bit like the ones in the drawing room at Lissadell, but apart from that, nothing seemed right. It was a cold day, but the fire wasn't lighting – and hadn't even been cleaned from whenever it had been lit before. The rugs were rolled up along one wall and there were stacks of books and papers everywhere. Everything was covered with a light layer of dust. I don't like cleaning, but if there had been a duster nearby, I couldn't have resisted using it. Near the window, some of the furniture had been pushed aside, and in its place was a big machine with a wheel on one side, and lots of cogs and belts. On the floor beside it was a stack of posters.

'What's this?' I asked, touching the smooth edge of the wheel. 'There's all kinds of modern machinery

in the basement at Lissadell, but I've never seen anything like this before.'

'I heard Uncle Joss saying that Mother has her own printing press, but I thought he was exaggerating as usual.'

'But why would she want a printing press?'

'I suppose to print political pamphlets and things. Uncle Joss says she uses it to make trouble for herself.'

I had to smile. Sir Josslyn was Countess Markievicz's brother, and they didn't agree on very much. I picked up a poster which seemed to be telling Irish men not to join the British army, and remembered that Sir Josslyn had recently given a speech saying the exact opposite. They were both very clever people and I wondered who was right. I thought about taking one of the posters to show Sam, but then stopped myself. What if Harry saw it? Harry believed he was fighting for a good cause, to save the people of Belgium, and got badly injured doing so. Wouldn't he be

upset if he saw something like this? It was all very complicated.

* * *

After a long, long wait, we heard the sound of the front door slamming.

'Mother!' said Maeve, jumping up. 'At last!'

But when we went out, the hallway was empty. I saw a movement and looked through the small window by the door, and recognised the messy hair of the girl walking away from us towards the front gate.

'It's only Susan,' I said. 'She's going away. I wonder if she will come back at all.'

'I hope not,' said Maeve.

After Susan left, the house seemed very still and lonely. Maeve was quiet and seemed sad. I tried to cheer her up, but nothing I said seemed to work, so in the end I sat quietly too.

'Are you hungry?' Maeve asked after a while.

'I thought you'd never ask!'

Maeve got up and rang the bell over the fireplace, but neither of us was surprised when no one came.

'Any food left in that basket?' I asked.

'Sorry. We only left a few crumbs. We're growing girls, you know.'

'Well, I'll stop growing if I don't get something to eat soon. Do you think your mother will be much longer?'

Maeve didn't answer, but I saw her wipe her eyes quickly, as if she hoped I wouldn't see the tears that were starting to form.

'Oh, Maeve,' I said. 'I'm sorry. I didn't mean to ...'

'It's all right,' she said with a watery smile. 'Let's see if we can find something to eat.'

We went out to the hall, tiptoeing on the tiles.

'The kitchen must be at the back, where we saw Susan go.'

She was whispering, as if we were trespassers or

criminals or something, though this was Maeve's Mam's own house.

The kitchen had lots of cupboards and a big larder, but most of the shelves were bare, except for stale crumbs and greasy stains. Once again, I thought of Lissadell House, where there was plenty of delicious food for everyone. Once again, I wondered why the countess chose to live in this strange, dirty house, when all the luxury and beauty of Lissadell could have been hers.

Maeve found a loaf of not-very-fresh-bread, and some butter, and when I came across a lump of hard cheese we celebrated as if we'd discovered treasure. Using a very blunt knife, we made the best sandwiches we could, and put them on a tray, with two glasses of cold water. Then we carried our feast back to the room where we'd been before, and ate every single scrap.

Chapter Thirteen

It was getting dark. I lit one of the gaslights, as Maeve didn't know how, though she'd grown up in a house with so many of them. Still there was no sign of Countess Markievicz. I wondered if she'd forgotten that Maeve was coming on a visit. What if she'd gone away for the night – or even for a week?

The room was cold. I thought about lighting a fire, but hadn't seen any wood or coal anywhere. I sighed as I thought of the huge coal store at Lissadell, with enough to heat every room of that huge house. Maeve went to fetch our coats, and a few other things from the hall stand. We wrapped them around our shoulders and legs making ourselves as cosy as possible. I was jealous when Poppet jumped onto Maeve's lap, helping to keep her knees warm. The regular ticking of the mantelpiece clock was lulling me to sleep, and

I was already half-dreaming of my warm bed at Lissadell.

'Lily?'

'What is it?' I asked sitting up straight, fully awake again and remembering where I was. 'Is your mother here?'

'No. No one's here but us two. I didn't tell you the full truth before. There's something important ... something ... I need to tell you ... about ... our trip here.'

'That's all right,' I said. 'I already know what's going on.'

'You do?'

'Yes. I worked it out while we were on the train. It's been decided that you're going to boarding school – and you've come to say goodbye to your mother before you leave. I know you must be sad, and I'm sorry for you. I'm glad I'm here, and I'll keep you company on the way home too. You must be brave. Summer won't be long coming and then you'll be

back to us for the holidays, I hope. You can ...'

Maeve started to shake her head slowly. 'No,' she said. 'No, Lily, you've got this all wrong. I'm *not* going to boarding school.'

I was cold and tired, and my head was muddled.

'Then why are we here?' I asked.

'I've come on a mission.'

'A mission?'

'Yes. I've come to ask Mother to change Gaga's mind about sending me to boarding school.'

I rubbed my eyes, trying to think clearly. 'But if Gaga has made up her mind about this, why did she and Lady Mary allow you to come here on this mission? If you're successful, what they want won't happen, and that doesn't make any sense. Why would they?'

'It's ... you see, there's one more thing I need to tell you about this trip – and it's a bit important. Lily, when you and I got on the train in Sligo ...'

She stopped talking as we heard the rattle of keys

and then the slam of the front door. I heard quick, firm steps in the hallway, and I knew this wasn't Susan the maid, whose steps were much slower and lazier.

The steps passed the room we were in, and I heard them starting up the stairs, when Poppet jumped out of Maeve's arms and ran to the door with one loud bark. Maeve and I stood up, leaving a puddle of coats and wraps at our feet. The steps stopped, and then came back down the stairs and along the hall towards us. I heard a woman's voice.

'Poppet. Where are you, my pet?'

I'd only heard this voice a few times before, but it was one I'd never forget.

Countess Markievicz was here!

* * *

The door opened a little and Poppet ran out to her mistress. The door began to close again, when Maeve

spoke. 'Mother. It's me. I'm here.'

Now the door opened fully, and I could see the countess. As always, she looked like a vision – tall and beautiful, and dressed in a simple, long black dress. Maeve and I stood side by side, and the countess stared at us, as if she couldn't believe her eyes.

Why did she look so surprised? I knew she was a busy woman, but could you be so busy that you'd forget your own girl was coming to stay?

'Maeve?' she said. 'And …?'

'It's Lily, Madame,' I said. 'Lily from Lissadell.' The countess nodded at me, but I couldn't tell if she remembered me from before.

Maeve took a step towards her mother, and I thought of the huge hugs my own lovely mam always greeted me with. These two were different though – they just stared at each other as if they weren't fully convinced that the other one existed.

'Why didn't your grandmother tell me you were coming?' asked the countess. 'If she sent a telegram, I

didn't see it. That Susan is a careless girl but even she wouldn't ignore a telegram. If I'd known about your arrival, I could have met you at the station, or sent someone to do so.'

I looked at my friend. Her face was blank, as if none of this surprised her. And then, all of a sudden, the truth came to me! Maeve and I had travelled all the way across the country, and no one knew at all where we were going. This trip wasn't only a surprise for me – it was a surprise for everyone except Maeve. She had tricked me.

Chapter Fourteen

People always said how wild and unconventional Countess Markievicz was – she often did what was unexpected, and didn't seem to care how people saw her. For a minute that gave me a little bit of hope. Maybe she'd laugh at what Maeve and I had done, or even admire us for undertaking such a trip without any adults to help us along the way. Maybe she'd pat us on the backs and say she'd have done exactly the same when she was a girl.

I was wrong.

The countess didn't shout at us, but her voice was loud and cross, and it terrified me. She marched up and down the room talking about the dangers for young girls travelling on their own. She talked about inconvenience for the adults in our lives. She talked for a very long time about how important her own

work was, and how she didn't have time to waste sorting out all the trouble we had caused. None of what she said recognised how sad and lonely her girl was, and how hard it was for Maeve living so far away from her mother.

Eventually the countess asked a question. 'Tell me, Maeve, why did you do this? Why did you sneak away from Sligo and come here? You have to tell me because I truly cannot work it out for myself. I have absolutely no idea what this madcap trip is all about.'

If I hadn't been so afraid, I'd have laughed. It was true, the countess probably couldn't guess the exact truth, but wouldn't she have guessed that her daughter missed her? Wouldn't that alone have been enough to make this journey happen?

Maeve was pale and silent, and I could see tears brimming in her eyes. Her mother asked the question again.

'Can you please explain to me why you are here?'

Maeve gave a big sigh. 'I suppose it's time to tell

you. We're here because ...'

The countess was still pacing up and down, looking as angry as ever, and I realised it wasn't a good time for this conversation. If Maeve told the truth now, the countess might put her on a boat to England immediately, and never allow her back to Lissadell again. Maybe in the morning she'd be calmer and more sympathetic. Maybe in the morning there was a chance that Maeve's plan might actually work.

I shook my head at Maeve, to make her stop talking, and then gave a huge yawn that was only half fake, as I had been up for so many hours. I sank onto an armchair, as if I couldn't stand up for another second.

The countess ran over and touched my forehead. 'Are you unwell, child?' she asked.

'No, Madame,' I said quickly. 'I'm perfectly well, thank you, but I'm very, very tired. I wonder if there is somewhere Maeve and I could sleep – and then we could all have a nice chat in the morning? Maeve and

I are both very sorry for any trouble we have caused, aren't we Maeve?'

'Oh yes,' said Maeve. 'We really are very sorry.'

'Oh,' said the countess, as if she had just realised something. 'Everyone at Lissadell must be worried about you two – and your family must be worried also, Lily.'

Mam! With all the excitement, I hadn't even thought about her. As far as she was concerned, I was tucked up in my bed at Lissadell. What would she say if she knew the truth?

'Actually, they're not worried,' said Maeve quietly.

'How can you know that?' asked her mother.

'Because I left a note on my bed, saying where we were going. I'm sure it will have been found by now, so everyone will know we are here with you. That means they won't be worried – and if they're not worried, they won't go sending messages to Lily's family either.'

That made me feel a small bit better – though I

was still terrified by what I'd become mixed up in.

For the first time, her mother looked a little less angry. 'I'm glad to hear you did that, Maeve,' she said. 'But things aren't so simple. Your note shows your intentions, but it doesn't say that you got here safely. I shall have to send a telegram to Lissadell to tell everyone you are well and here with me.'

Maeve and I followed the countess to the hallway, watching as she took a coat from the stand, and put it on, not noticing that it was made for a man – who was smaller than her.

'It might be too late to send a telegram now,' she sighed. 'But I can arrange for it to be sent first thing in the morning, which is the best I can do. I don't know how long I'll be, so you two girls should go to bed.'

'Where?' asked Maeve, which was a fair question, as at the top of the stairs I could see a number of rooms, and then the stairs turned back on itself, suggesting that there were more rooms on another level.

The countess waved her hand in the air. 'Oh, just find somewhere. There's a lot of coming and going in this house, so the beds should all be made up. Mine's the room with the blue door, so don't pick that one please.'

Then she went out and disappeared into the night.

Chapter Fifteen

The house had lots of bedrooms. In some of them, it was hard to see the bed for all the books and paintings piled up on the floor. I couldn't resist looking into the room with the blue door, and was disappointed to see that it looked just like all the others. Everything was dusty and untidy, and as far from Countess Markievicz's bedroom at Lissadell as it was possible to be.

In the end, Maeve picked a room that looked a tiny bit cleaner than the others, and because neither of us felt like being alone, we snuggled up together in the small bed, and settled down for the night.

* * *

'Maeve?' I was whispering, though except for us, the

house was empty.

'What?' she whispered. I heard her turning over in the bed so we were facing each other in the dark.

'I've got lots of questions for you.'

'Oh, Lily. It's very late. Couldn't we wait until morning? Couldn't we ...?'

Now I felt angry as well as scared. Maeve had tricked me. Maybe she could sense my anger as she changed her tune. 'Of course,' she said. 'Ask me anything you wish.'

I started with an easy question. 'Cook didn't know anything about this trip, so why did she give you such a big basket of food?'

'Oh, I told her you and I were going to have a picnic – only I didn't say it was going to be on a train on the way to Dublin. Cook didn't mind anyway – you know how she likes to make up baskets for us.'

'Lady Mary must have noticed the basket. Didn't she wonder what it was for? You weren't likely to be having a picnic in the middle of Sligo Town.'

'Maybe she did notice, but she didn't ask me anything about it. Aunt Mary feels sorry for me, so she's being extra-nice at the moment.'

Lady Mary is one of the kindest women in the world, so that made sense.

Now I had a harder question to ask. Part of me wanted to shout it out – *your granny thinks you should go to boarding school because you're always in trouble, and 'running wild around the country' – so you try to avoid it by getting into more trouble, and running wild all the way to Dublin? What kind of a plan is that?*

This mad, secret trip to Dublin might have made things a whole lot worse, but my friend was sad and lonely and scared, and I didn't want to upset her anymore. 'Did you really think this plan was going to work?' I asked gently.

For a long time she didn't answer, and I wondered if she'd fallen asleep.

'Yes … no … I'm not sure. Oh, Lily, I didn't even think too hard about what I was going to do. This

isn't something I've been planning for a long time. The whole idea only came to me yesterday when Gaga came back to Lissadell. When I heard she was going to write to Mother, I was so sad and upset and ... I dread going to boarding school ... maybe in a year or two I wouldn't mind ... but now I'm too young. I'm too afraid! All I could think was that if I told Mother how scared I was, maybe she wouldn't make me go. Then when Aunt Mary suggested a trip to Sligo Town – that made everything easy.'

And then I understood. I wasn't part of a big, complicated scheme – I was watching the sad acts of a desperate and lonely girl.

'Why didn't you tell me this morning what you were planning to do?' I asked.

'If I told you – would you have come?'

I didn't know the answer to her question.

'I love you, Maeve,' I said. 'But ...'

Now she began to cry. 'I'm sorry,' she said. 'I'm so sorry for dragging you into this whole mess – it

was a stupid idea. Mother is very cross with me, so it doesn't look as if my plan will even work.'

'My mam says things always seem better in the light of morning,' I said, as I took her hand. 'Maybe tomorrow your mother will have calmed down a bit, and we can talk to her.'

'*We* can talk to her? Oh, Lily, thank you so much. Thank you for helping me with this. Mother likes to get up early so we'd better get up early too – so we can chat to her before she goes out.'

I felt a sick feeling in my stomach. Why had I said that? I like helping my friends, but there's a limit to what I can do. How was a young housemaid like me supposed to take on a countess? And her mother? If they wanted Maeve to go to boarding school, how could I possibly make them change their minds?

Chapter Sixteen

a barking dog interrupted my dreams.

'Mam? What's ...?'

I jumped up in fright. It was already light. Why hadn't Nellie called me? Why hadn't the clattering of pans from the kitchen woken me before dawn the way they usually did?

Then I saw Maeve slumbering next to me, as if she hadn't a care in the world. Mam says a problem shared is a problem halved – but I wasn't sure if Maeve's problem had been shared equally. I felt as if Benbulben was resting on my shoulders.

Then Maeve opened her eyes. She smiled when she saw me sitting in the bed next to her, and for a second I felt angry again. Was this whole thing only a bit of fun to her? But as I watched, her smile faded, and I knew she was remembering where she was, and

why. *She* knew how much trouble she was in. *I* knew it was up to me to save her.

* * *

We straightened our clothes as best we could, and Maeve peeped into the hallway. The door to her mother's room was open, and I was relieved to see it was empty. Maeve ran across and returned with a beautiful silver hairbrush. We took turns brushing each other's hair, which was nice. Maeve took a long time doing mine, and I guessed this was deliberate. She was delaying the moment when she'd have to talk to her mother.

'Stop!' I said in the end, taking the brush from her. 'I don't want to spend the rest of my life in this room, too afraid to go downstairs.'

'I suppose you're right,' she sighed. 'Let's go and face the music.'

* * *

Our footsteps slowed as we got to the bottom of the stairs. I could hear angry men's voices coming from the room where we'd been the night before. What was going on? Was this because of Maeve and me? Had we broken some kind of law by travelling on our own? Was the room full of policemen come to take us to jail?

Then the door opened, and Susan came out carrying a tray stacked with a wobbly tower of dirty cups and plates.

'Madame is hosting an important political meeting,' she said when she saw us. 'So she has no time to make breakfast for you.'

I smiled. I was very happy to hear that Madame's visitors had nothing to do with Maeve and me – and the thought of a countess making breakfast for a housemaid was hilarious. Then my smile faded. Saving the world is important, but didn't the coun-

tess *ever* put her own girl first?

Maeve and I followed Susan to the kitchen, where she waved at a board with half a loaf of bread and some cheese, making me wonder if that's all they ate in this strange house. At that moment I'd have given a lot for one of Cook's custard tarts, or a slice of her still-warm home-made bread.

'You can help yourselves, I suppose,' said Susan. 'And you can eat at the table over there.'

Maeve and I took some food and carried it to the table Susan had indicated. She didn't seem to think it strange for a young lady like Maeve to be eating in the kitchen like a servant. Once again, I wondered what kind of a house this was at all.

'Madame said she'll talk to you when the meeting is over,' said Susan

'When will that be?' asked Maeve.

'I don't know, do I?' said Susan. 'Some of her meetings go on all day, and into the night too. Sometimes people sleep wherever they can find a space, and then

get up in the morning and it starts all over again. It's not easy for me, I can tell you.'

The girl was unfriendly, but for the first time I felt some sympathy for her. How was she supposed to work amidst this kind of chaos? How was she supposed to manage the whole house all on her own? How different *my* work was, with Mrs Bailey and her lists and plans and her schedule of who would be where and when. Maybe my life at Lissadell wasn't so bad after all.

When Maeve and I had eaten, we sat in the corner of the kitchen, watching as Susan slowly washed some of the many dirty cups and plates. Maeve and I didn't talk, and as I watched the clock over the fireplace, every minute ticking slowly by felt like an hour. After a while I went over to Susan at the sink.

'I could help you with that,' I said, looking at the greasy brown water. 'The two of us could get it done quickly, and then ...'

'I *don't* need your help,' she snapped, looking a little

bit afraid. 'You're a guest in this house.'

'Well, I suppose I am a guest,' I said. 'But I'm also ...'

Now Susan looked at me more closely, as if she'd just noticed that, even though I was wearing my best clothes, I was very shabby compared to Maeve.

'Who *are* you?' she asked. 'Are you after my job or what? Because if you are, I can tell you that's not going to happen. Madame has no complaints about my work – and she knows how my family needs the money I bring home.'

The poor girl was trapped in this awful job, and was terrified of losing it. 'I was only trying to be nice,' I said. 'If you don't want my help, that's all right too. I'll just sit here with Maeve, until ...'

I was interrupted by the sound of footsteps in the hall, and calls of 'goodbye' and 'see you next week.' There was a loud slam of the front door, and then silence.

'The meeting is over,' whispered Maeve. 'I wonder

if we should ...'

Before she could finish, the kitchen door opened and the countess stood in front of us. Her hair was untidy and she had a streak of ink on her cheek. There was also a strange wild look in her eyes.

'Come to the drawing room, Maeve,' she said. 'You and I need to have a talk.'

Even though Maeve had been expecting this, her face went pale, and I could see that her hands were shaking. She was afraid of her own mother!

Maeve stood up and took my hand in hers. 'I want Lily to come too,' she said.

The countess stared as if she'd only just noticed I was there.

'As you wish,' she said. 'Follow me.'

So, with Maeve's fingers holding mine so tightly it hurt, we followed her mother, so we could have a conversation that would very likely change Maeve's life.

Chapter Seventeen

Maeve and I sat together on a small couch and waited. Her mother seemed distracted by a bundle of pamphlets that lay on a table. She shuffled through them, sighing a bit and shaking her head. Then she picked up a jotter and began to write. She wrote for a long time, and when she put the jotter down, I could see it was some kind of letter, signed at the bottom in a scrawl I recognised. I thought of the small room at Lissadell, where the young countess had signed her name on the glass. Somehow this made me feel a bit better. This scary woman had once been young too. Once she had childish hopes and dreams. Could she remember this, and take some pity on her only girl?

Finally the countess turned to us.

'I have received a telegram from Lissadell,' she said.

'Everyone knows you are safe with me, so there was no need to send any messages to your family, Lily.'

This was great news. At least my poor mam wouldn't be worrying about me.

'Thank you, Madame,' I whispered.

Now the countess turned to Maeve. 'The telegram isn't the only thing I received this morning,' she said. 'There was also a letter – from Gaga. I expect you know what it was about.'

Maeve nodded.

'It appears you've been nothing but trouble lately,' said her mother. 'As I can see by your unannounced arrival here! Your grandmother is too old for this kind of thing, and as for poor Miss Clayton, what did she ever do to deserve such treatment? What have you got to say for yourself, young lady?'

'I'm sorry,' whispered Maeve. 'I'll behave from now on – I promise.'

'That's not quite good enough,' said her mother. 'Gaga says you have made many promises already –

163

promises you have broken.'

'I won't break this promise – I ... promise,' said Maeve. 'My behaviour will be exemplary from now on. Just give me a chance, Mother. Please give me a chance. Don't send me away to boarding school. I would hate that so much. I would ...'

Maeve kept talking. She was begging and pleading, but soon she was crying so hard, I couldn't make out much of what she was saying. My mam knows that we children are mostly good, so she gives us lots of chances, but when I looked at the countess, I didn't feel hopeful. The newspapers were always telling stories of how kind this woman was, but now she was standing over her own daughter, looking as if she had a heart of stone. I had a horrible feeling that Maeve was wasting her time. I had a horrible feeling that the countess's mind was already made up, and that Maeve would soon be packing up her belongings for a new life in England.

Then I remembered something Maeve had said

the night before, and I decided to take a chance.

'Maeve is still very young, Madame,' I said. 'She thinks she's too young to go all the way to England on her own.'

'It seems she's not too young to go to from Sligo to Dublin on her own, is she?' said her mother. That made me angry. Was she mocking Maeve? Was she ignoring the fact that Maeve wasn't on her own on the journey to Dublin – that she had me with her?

Then the countess smiled, and her smile was very charming and my anger faded away. I could see how this woman managed to give speeches that made people change their minds, and do things they'd have been afraid to do before.

'If you could wait two years maybe?' I looked at Maeve and she nodded through her tears, telling me it was all right to continue like this. The poor girl was so upset, she would have agreed to any kind of delay at all. 'In two years,' I continued. 'Maeve wouldn't be so afraid of moving away. She'd go to boarding

school without any complaint at all.'

'Lily's right,' sobbed Maeve. 'Please, Mother. Please let me stay in Sligo for another two years, and after that, I'll do anything you wish – I promise.'

Now, for the first time, the countess looked unsure.

'I really don't know how to respond,' she said. 'You have been running wild around the countryside, Maeve, and I am afraid that will get worse. In two years' time, you might be too wild for any boarding school. It could be like sending an unbroken pony to compete in the Dublin Horse Show.'

Now I smiled. I'd once overheard Gaga saying that when the countess was young, she behaved like an unbroken pony. Maybe Maeve's only crime was being too like her mother.

'Please,' whispered Maeve. 'You're my mother. If you say I can wait two years, Gaga will have to agree.'

'I have to think of Miss Clayton,' said the countess. 'You know the rights of workers are very important to me.'

I thought of poor Susan slaving away, trying to keep a big house going all on her own. Didn't the countess care about the worker who was right there in front of her?

'Miss Clayton is good, and hard-working,' continued the countess. 'And she doesn't deserve the way you have been treating her. The poor woman is only trying to make a living for herself.'

And then I had one of the best ideas of my life.

'Can I ask you a question, please, Madame?' I said.

The countess nodded, so I went on.

'If Maeve goes to boarding school, what will happen to Miss Clayton?'

'She will have to find another position,' said the countess. 'Unfortunately, that is the lot of a governess – when their charges grow up, their job is done.'

'So she will lose her home and her job at the same time? Where will she go? How will she live? Maybe she will starve.'

The countess sniffed. 'I would of course pay her

wages for a few weeks while she searches for a new posting. She shall have an excellent reference from me so I'm sure it won't take long.'

'But there's a war on,' I said. 'And things are changing all the time. Maybe Miss Clayton won't be able to find a job, but if …'

The countess stared at me with narrowed eyes. 'Do tell me more, Lily,' she said.

'If you let Maeve stay in Sligo for two more years, Miss Clayton will have a job for all that time.'

'But she will still have to leave in the end,' said the countess. 'We can't have her with us forever.'

'Maybe not forever,' I said. 'But in two years, Miss Bridget will need a governess at Lissadell, and after that there will be little Rosaleen. If Lady Mary keeps on having babies, Miss Clayton could have a job for a very long time. You said she's good and hard-working, so if she stays, everyone will be happy.'

The countess stared at me. 'Lily, I have to say you are a very impressive young lady,' she said. 'Have you

thought about a future in politics?'

I laughed, thinking she was joking. 'But politics is only for men,' I said. 'Women and girls can't even vote.'

'Ah yes,' said the countess. 'That is true. But things are changing, and the war will make the rate of change speed up even more. Maybe you should stay here in Dublin with me. I could find you work as a housemaid, and when you're old enough maybe ...?'

As she spoke, a glimpse of an exciting new life opened up in front of me, but then I shook my head. I'd gone to all this trouble to keep Maeve in Sligo, so why would I now stay in Dublin?

How could I live so far away from Nellie, and Mam, and my little brothers and sisters?

How could I survive with all the loud busyness of this huge city?

'Thank you,' I said. 'But I'd like to return to Sligo.'

'And be a housemaid for the rest of your life?'

'No! I mean ... being a housemaid is a good job,

and I'm grateful for all the Gore-Booths do for me, but I hope to be a teacher one day.'

'I can see you will be a very good teacher,' said the countess. 'The children will be lucky to have you.'

I could feel myself glowing from having this fine woman saying such nice things about me, and this made me brave.

'So, is it settled that Maeve will stay at Lissadell for two more years?' I asked.

Next to me, my friend stopped wiping her red eyes, as we both held our breath waiting for her mother to answer.

The countess looked at us for a long time, and then she gave a big sigh. 'Yes,' she said. 'It is settled. But if there is any more serious misbehaviour, Maeve, you will be off to boarding school before you have time to even think about it – and no begging from you or this persuasive friend of yours will change things.'

'I understand, Mother,' said Maeve.

'Very well,' said the countess. 'I shall write to Gaga

this evening and let her know.'

I wanted to hug her, but since her own daughter didn't do that, it might have seemed a bit strange.

Instead, Maeve jumped up and down a bit, and her eyes shone as she repeated, 'thank you, thank you, thank you,' over and over again. I wasn't sure if the words were meant for me or her mother, but I didn't care. Maeve's wish to stay in Sligo was really coming true!

* * *

Now the doorbell rang, and a second later Susan came in. I looked at her sullen face and her dirty uniform, and thought again of how different Lissadell was, with its footmen and a butler and a whole team of other servants.

'There's two men and a woman outside, Madame,' said Susan. 'They say you're going to an important meeting together.'

The countess looked at her wristwatch, and gave a little cry. 'I'm so very late,' she said. 'Could you get my coat and hat for me please, Susan?'

Susan sighed as she turned and left the room, as if she'd been asked to walk all the way to Belfast, instead of just out to the hallstand. The countess was muttering names and addresses to herself as she began to follow her.

'Mother?' said Maeve. 'What should Lily and I do?'

The countess stopped at the door, and turned to face us. The expression on her face made me think she was so preoccupied with her meeting that she'd forgotten all about us.

'Oh,' she said. 'My meeting could last a few hours, so I suppose you should wait here for now. As soon as I can, I'll send someone to bring you to the railway station for your journey home. Goodbye.'

Then with a wave of her hand, she left the room, closing the door behind her.

This was her only child!

This was her girl who'd broken all kinds of rules, and crossed the country to plead with her!

What meeting could be more important than spending a little bit of time together?

If I were a different girl, a very strong and brave one, I'd have run after the countess and given her a big shake – and maybe even a slap too. But I'm not quite as brave as that, so I turned to my friend, and smiled, pretending I couldn't see how hurt she was.

She gave a small smile back, joining in the pretence.

'At least I'm not going to boarding school for another few years,' she said.

And then we listened as the front door of the house slammed loudly. The countess had left.

Chapter Eighteen

Maeve and I sat in silence for a long time. I had a funny mix of feelings.

I was glad I'd helped her.

I was sorry her mother was so cold.

I felt guilty for liking the countess, despite this coldness.

I felt sad that I was being sent back to Sligo without getting a chance to see more of this big, exciting city.

The windows towards the street were slightly open. I listened to the footsteps outside, trying to decide which belonged to men and women, and which to children. I wondered who all these people were, and where they could be going.

Then I heard the squeak of the front gate, and steps coming towards the house. I couldn't get excited. It

was probably a delivery boy, or some other messenger. Maybe it was someone coming to ask the countess to go to *another* meeting.

Then I heard the rattle of keys, and the sound of the front door opening, and a second later, the countess was in the room with us.

'I came back,' she said.

I thought she'd probably forgotten her gloves, or one of the many pamphlets lying around the room, but then she continued.

'I have put off the meeting until tomorrow. My daughter doesn't visit every day, so we have to make an event of it. What would you like to do, Maeve?'

I turned to Maeve and it was like watching the sun come out after weeks of rain.

'I ... I ... I ...'

Maeve was more flustered than I'd ever seen her before, and I understood she didn't care what she did. She'd have been happy to sit forever in the untidy room, being in the presence of her mother, knowing

she wanted them to spend time together.

I had *lots* of ideas, but unfortunately, no one was asking me.

'Very well, said her mother. 'I shall have to decide for all of us. Get your coats, girls, we are going out.'

* * *

The three of us walked along Leinster Road together. At first, I hung back, thinking it right for me to be a few steps behind, but Maeve caught my hand and pulled me level. This made all the difference, as I held my head up, looking at everything, and wondering how I could remember every single detail to tell my brothers later. I wasn't a fine lady, but I could act like one for a little while, and that was good enough for me.

Everyone we passed greeted the countess like an old friend. One woman in ragged clothes rushed up and took her hands and held on as if she were

drowning. 'Oh, Madame,' she said. 'Thank you for the medicine. My Daniel's cough is better now, and soon he'll be able to go back to work. May you be rewarded for your kindness.'

Another lady thanked her for a parcel of food, and a man said the blanket she'd given him made all the difference to his sick mother.

Now I understood why the countess didn't mind Maeve being friends with a housemaid. She didn't think about whether people were rich or poor – she just treated everyone the same.

'I'm glad I could help,' said the countess to them all, looking a little embarrassed. I thought Maeve might be embarrassed too, but I could see she was delighted so many people seemed to know and like her mother. Soon she was almost skipping along.

'Where are we going?' asked Maeve after a while.

'Oh, I thought I could show you some of the historical buildings and monuments near here,' said her mother.

'That would be wonderful!' said Maeve. 'Thank you, Mother.'

I turned to see if my friend was all right. (She's always complaining about how boring history is, and how Miss Clayton makes her study it deliberately, just to annoy her). Maeve was beaming though, and I knew all she wanted was to be near her mother.

'You'd like that too, wouldn't you Lily?' said the countess.

I tried to smile. I loved being in the city, but looking at buildings and monuments wouldn't have been high on my list of exciting things to do.

Maybe my smile wasn't convincing enough, as the countess stopped walking and stared at us both.

'I don't spend much time with girls your age,' she said. 'So, I might have got this wrong. What would you really like to do?'

Maeve didn't answer so I knew it was up to me. The only trouble was I didn't dare to suggest anything.

'Oh, you girls!' said the countess with a smile.

'Obviously the world is too full of possibility for you. I have a good idea, so come along before we run out of time.'

The countess had long legs, and as she marched ahead with her silk scarf streaming out behind her, Maeve and I had to almost run to keep up with her.

Soon we arrived at the gates of a large park. I could smell frying food and sweet cake, and I could hear the sound of music and laughter. It looked as if the whole of Dublin was there, with couples strolling arm in arm, and children darting in and out of the crowds, laughing and shouting.

'It's a carnival,' said the countess. 'I'm too old for this kind of thing, but I believe young people enjoy it. I'm going to rest on this bench here, and you two can have some fun. I'll be here if you need me.'

She reached into her pocket and gave Maeve a few coins. Maeve took my hand and led me into the crowd, and I thought I would surely faint away from the excitement of it all.

'What would you like to do first?' asked Maeve.

I gazed at all the loud and beautiful attractions, and, for once in my life, I was almost speechless. 'Everything!' I whispered in the end, and Maeve laughed.

'Everything it is then. Come along, and let's get started.'

We went on the carousel and the swinging boats. We watched a puppet show, and peeped into a tent to see the world's tallest man. We saw a woman who looked as if she had a beard made of bees. We watched a man juggling with fire. We ate candy floss and roasted chestnuts and other things I didn't even know the name of. After a while, we ran back to where the countess was sitting on a bench, already best friends with the old lady sitting next to her.

'Go and enjoy yourselves,' she said. 'There's another half hour before we have to leave.'

I could see that Maeve was undecided. She wanted to spend time with her mother, but the excitement of

the carnival was tempting too.

'Go!' said the countess, and so we went, running and laughing and enjoying ourselves.

'Oh look,' I said after a while. 'Can we go in there?'

Maeve turned to where I was pointing at a small, brightly-coloured tent, with a sign outside – *Fortune Teller.*

Maeve paid a man, and we stepped inside the tent, which was warm and a bit smelly. An old woman sat on a stool, and she smiled when she saw us.

'Who wants to know the future?'

Maeve pushed me forward. 'Lily does!' she said, giggling.

The woman took my hand and turned it over and back, as if she could see something there. Her hands were dry and looked as if they hadn't been washed for a while. Then she fanned out some cards and asked me to take one.

I reached for a few before making up my mind. With a shaking hand, I picked out the card closest

to me, turned it over and read the words written in gold ink.

All your dreams will come true

The old woman smiled as she put the card on the table beside her. 'Lucky girl,' she said. 'You picked a good card.' I wanted to kiss her grubby cheek. Did she know how badly I wanted to be a teacher? Did the card mean it was really going to happen?

I stepped away and pushed Maeve towards the woman. 'Your turn,' I said.

Like me, Maeve spent a long time choosing a card. Like me, she had lots of hopes and wishes and wanted to know how her life was going to turn out. But when she turned her card over, it had the exact same words on it. *All your dreams will come true.*

Of course I wanted Maeve to be happy, but if the two cards were the same ...?

Now Maeve started to laugh, which didn't please the old woman, who snatched the card from her hand. As she did so, the whole bundle fell to the

floor. I hurried to pick them up, but stopped when I saw that each card had the exact same words on it. I felt angry. The old woman was a fake. But when Maeve saw the cards, she began to laugh even more, and I couldn't help joining in, and we laughed until the man outside came to see what was happening, and he chased us out of the tent, and Maeve and I ran away hand in hand, and the man shouted after us and I didn't care because I was in Dublin with my friend and everything was fine.

Chapter Nineteen

'*A*nyone hungry?'

Even though I'd eaten so much at the carnival, the countess's words made my mouth water. Maybe fun and excitement make you hungry?

'I'm starving,' said Maeve.

'Me too,' I said.

The countess checked her wristwatch. 'There's some time before I have to bring you to the railway station,' she said. 'Let's go and have some tea.'

I'd been to a tea room and even a hotel in Sligo before, but the hotel the countess took us to was fancier than any I could have imagined. The three of us walked up some shiny marble steps, and a man in a uniform opened a door for us, bowing and greeting us like royalty. My best clothes were much shabbier than anything anyone else was wearing (and I'd slept

in them!), but as I was with the countess, no one seemed to mind.

'Countess!' said a man in a fine dark blue suit. 'So nice to see you, and your lovely young companions too. Come with me and I'll find you a nice table by the window.'

As we followed him, I didn't know what to enjoy next. My feet sank deep into the rich red carpet, my hands brushed the embossed wallpaper, and I listened to the sweet piano music coming from a corner of the room. For a moment I felt sad for my poor mam, whose life has been so hard, and who never even dreams of nice things like this.

When we were seated on chairs with the fattest cushions I'd ever seen, a waitress came over. She was wearing a black and white uniform, a little like the one I wear at Lissadell.

'Madame!' she said, bending low and almost bowing to the countess. 'Such an honour to have you with us again.'

'Hello, Agnes,' said the countess. 'How are you? And how is your husband?'

'Oh, Madame,' she said. 'He is almost himself again. Since you got him that job in the coal yard office, he's a new man. He smiles all the time, and we don't have to worry about paying the bills or feeding the children. You're an angel – you truly are!'

The countess waved her hand in the air. 'It was nothing at all, and I'm happy to hear it is all working out well. Now what can you recommend for my daughter and her friend?'

Agnes brought us sandwiches with big thick slices of beef, and plates of salad, and bowls of soup, and cups of tea and milk and fizzy drinks that tickled my nose.

We ate as much as we could, and when Agnes heard that Maeve and I were travelling back to Sligo, she took the leftovers and packaged them up for our journey home. Maeve placed them carefully in Cook's basket, and then the countess, her daughter

and I sat back on our comfy seats and chatted like three rich friends on a normal afternoon out.

* * *

The railway station wasn't so scary this time. Maybe I was getting used to the bustle of Dublin, or maybe it was because the countess was striding along in front of Maeve and me, confidently buying tickets and finding the train we needed, and escorting us to our seats, and sitting facing us as we waited.

There was a loud whistle and the countess jumped up. 'That's my signal,' she said. 'If I'm not off this train in one minute, I'll have to go to Sligo with you.'

'I'd like that,' said Maeve quietly.

The countess put her hand on Maeve's shoulder. 'I know you would, darling,' she said. 'But I have work to do here, and I must stay.'

I could see tears beginning to form in Maeve's eyes, but she fought them back. 'I understand, Mother,'

she said. 'Thank you for a lovely day – and thank you for saying I can stay in Sligo for another two years.'

'Don't make me regret my decision,' said her mother, then the sound of another whistle made her run for the door. 'I've sent a telegram,' she said. 'So someone will meet you at the station.'

'Thank you, Madame,' I called after her. 'Thank you so much.'

The countess stood on the platform, and Maeve and I waved until she was only a small grey dot in the distance. I thought Maeve might cry, the way I would if I were leaving my mam, with no idea when I'd see her again, but she sat up straight in her seat and did her best to smile. I patted her arm. Poor Maeve, always saying goodbye to her mother.

* * *

The journey to Sligo seemed to take a very long time. We watched out the window as the wonders

of Dublin slipped away from us. We counted cows and waved at strangers. We ate the food Agnes had packed for us. Over and over again, Maeve said sorry for tricking me, and thanked me for saving her from boarding school for another while. Over and over again I told her she was welcome, and how happy I was to help.

* * *

'Lily, wake up. We're here. We're back in Sligo. I can see Albert waiting for us.'

I jumped up, bumping my head on the luggage rack. It was dark outside, and except for Maeve and me, the train seemed to be empty. I shivered as I pulled my coat tighter around me. We were almost home.

* * *

Maeve and I sat together in the back seat of the big motor car. Albert tucked a warm tartan blanket around us, but he didn't give us one of his big smiles. As we drove along, he didn't whistle and sing the way he usually did. I couldn't understand why the friendly man we knew so well was acting like this. I looked at Maeve, but she was staring out through the window, with a strange, sad look on her face. So we travelled along the windy roads in silence, which made me nervous, though I wasn't sure why.

'Here we are,' said Albert as he drove through the porte cochère.

Maeve and I stretched and went to get out of the car.

'Not you, Miss Maeve,' said Albert. 'I'm to take you to Ardeevin immediately – orders of your grandmother.'

'Oh!' was all Maeve said. Then she turned and hugged me, and thanked me one more time for my help.

I felt sorry for my friend as I climbed out of the car. Her mother might have saved her from boarding school for a while, but it didn't sound as if her grandmother was very happy. Then, as the car drove away, I began to feel sorry for myself too. The trip to Dublin had distracted me beautifully, but now all my worries came racing back.

What was going to happen to Sam?

Was I ever going to be a teacher?

Or was I going to be stuck cleaning floors and dusting furniture for the rest of my life?

The car lights faded away, and I turned to go up the steps, before remembering that, without Maeve, I'd no business entering the house by the front door. Squinting to see in the darkness I made my way to the servants' tunnel. My Dublin adventure was definitely over.

* * *

'Lily? Is that you? Are you back?'

Normally I'd have laughed at Nellie's last question but now I was too tired to manage even a little smile.

'Yes, it's me,' I whispered, as I fumbled in the dark for my nightgown. 'Go back to sleep.' Nellie and I get up before dawn, and work all the day long, so sleep was precious, but now she climbed from under her blankets and lit the gas light. Then she sat on her bed and stared at me as if she'd never seen me before.

'I missed you,' she said.

'But I was only gone for one night!'

'I know – but before we knew where you were, Johanna and I were so worried – everyone was. We had no idea what had happened to you. Until I went to Maeve's room and saw her note, it was as if you'd both vanished from the earth.'

'I'm sorry about that. You know I wouldn't deliberately upset or hurt you, don't you?'

She nodded, and her golden curls shone in the light of the gas flame.

'You see, what happened was ... Maeve ... she ...'
But then, I didn't want to make Maeve sound like a
bad person, so I changed my mind about what I was
going to say. 'Maeve is very upset about the thought
of boarding school,' I said. 'So I helped her talk to
her mother about it – and now she doesn't have to go
away for two years!'

'That's good news. It was kind of you to help her.'

Suddenly I wasn't tired any more. Now I wanted
to tell my friend about the wonderful time I'd had
in Dublin. 'Let me tell you about what Maeve and I
did,' I said. 'We got the train all on our own, and it
was very exciting. And then we had to get a tram to
the countess's house and ...'

I stopped talking. I was telling Nellie about the
best adventure I'd ever had, but she didn't seem interested, which didn't make any sense as she usually
loved to hear my stories. She might have been jealous, but that didn't make sense either, Nellie didn't
have a jealous bone in her body.

'Lily,' she said. Her face was so serious, I suddenly felt afraid. Had something terrible happened while I was away? Was Sam gone off to war? Was someone sick or hurt? Was it Johanna? Or Mam? Or one of my little brothers or sisters?

'What?' I said. 'Nellie, tell me why you're looking at me like that.'

'Oh, Lily. You're in terrible, terrible trouble.'

'But why?'

'For running away to Dublin on the train – and not telling anyone.'

And now I knew I had to tell my friend the truth.

'But *I* didn't do anything wrong. Maeve tricked me. She said the trip was a surprise for me – so when I got on the train, I thought everyone here knew where we were going.'

'And what happened when you found out the truth?'

'By then we were already in the countess's house, and there was nothing I could do. And poor Maeve

was so sad and upset, I couldn't really be cross with her.'

'I *knew* you wouldn't do anything to make us worry, and Johanna said the same. We guessed there had to be some kind of misunderstanding. When Mrs Bailey was angry, I tried to tell her that. I tried and tried, but she wouldn't listen.'

Nellie is a timid girl, and the thought of her facing up to Mrs Bailey to save me, made me love her even more than I had before.

I pulled on my nightgown and put out the light.

'Was Mrs Bailey very, very cross?' I asked as I got into bed.

'Yes,' said Nellie. 'Crosser than I've ever seen her before.'

'What did she say? Will I have to miss my day off to make up for the time I was away? I know that might seem fair to her, but I can't miss my only day in the week with Mam.'

Nellie didn't answer, and I felt a sudden sick feel-

ing in my tummy. 'She won't ... she didn't say ... I
mean, my job here ... did she say I might have to ...
leave? Nellie?'

'It's late, Lily pet,' she said. 'Let's go to sleep.'

This wasn't fair. The trip to Dublin wasn't my fault.
Why was *I* getting the blame?

And I lay there for hours, wondering what was
going to happen to me at all.

Chapter Twenty

'Lily. My office. Now!'

It was still dark. Nellie and I had dressed in silence, and were on our way to pick up our mops and brushes for the first jobs of the day.

'Yes, Mrs Bailey,' I said. Nellie squeezed my hand and gave me an encouraging smile. It was a bit late though – all the things she hadn't said the night before had me worried sick, and Mrs Bailey's sharp words didn't help.

The housekeeper closed the door firmly behind us. She sat at her desk, and though there was another chair, I didn't dare to sit on it. I fixed my cap and straightened my apron and then stood with my head down and my hands clasped in front of me, the way she'd taught me on my very first day at Lissadell, so long ago.

'Lily Brennan you are a disgrace!' said Mrs Bailey. Her voice was quiet, almost a whisper, but as cold as the water in the back kitchen on a frosty morning. 'I have been a housekeeper for twenty years and never, ever before has one of my housemaids behaved so badly.'

Grown-ups hate when you argue with them, but this was so wrong, I couldn't stop myself.

'That's not fair!' I said. 'None of this was my fault.'

'So, you're saying Miss Maeve dragged you kicking and screaming on to the train?'

'No – but ...'

'All that time rambling the countryside with Miss Maeve has turned your head, and this is the result. Today is Wednesday. You may stay and finish the week, and go home on Saturday as usual, but this time, you can bring all your belongings with you. At that stage your employment will be terminated, and you will not be expected back. It goes without saying you will not be receiving a reference from me

or anyone else at Lissadell House.'

'But you can't!'

'Don't you dare tell me what I can and can't do. This conversation is over. Now go upstairs and finish the work the Gore-Booths are paying you good money for.'

This was so unfair! I wanted to argue with Mrs Bailey. I wanted to protest, and tell her how wrong she was, but it was as if my brain was melting and I couldn't get any words out. Tears poured down my cheeks, but I couldn't make a sound. I turned and left the little office, closing the door quietly behind me.

* * *

'Oh, Lily dear, please stop crying,' said Nellie for the hundredth time, putting her arms around me.

'You'll make yourself ill,' said Johanna. 'And then where will you be?'

We were sitting on my bed, with a blanket wrapped

around the three of us. I had somehow made it through the day, letting my tears mix with the soapy water, as I scrubbed and cleaned as usual. I had barely touched my dinner or my tea, and now I felt weak and shaky.

'Try and be brave,' said Nellie. 'You always said you'd be leaving Lissadell one day – now this day has come a bit sooner than you expected.'

'But this isn't the way I hoped it would be,' I said. 'I thought when I left, everyone would be waving and hugging me and wishing me well. I didn't expect to be leaving in disgrace like this.'

'I'll still hug you and wave goodbye,' said Nellie fiercely. 'You'll never be in disgrace with me.'

'And the same goes for me,' said Johanna. 'And for Isabelle, and Delia and all your other friends. I know it's hard, and unfair, Lily, but when you're a teacher, this will be forgotten – it will be like a bad dream, meaning nothing at all.'

And at those words I cried harder and harder than

ever before, as I faced up to the thought I'd been avoiding all day.

'That's the worst part,' I sobbed. 'Mrs Bailey won't give me a reference, and without that, the Master can't give me a job as a teacher. No one will give me any kind of job at all. I'll have to live at home with Mam, and she'll have less money and an extra mouth to feed. She won't have all the treats Cook sends. My whole family could go hungry because of this – and none of it is even my fault.'

'You must go to Mrs Bailey and explain,' said Nellie. 'Tell her the truth about what happened.'

'You didn't see what she was like,' I said. 'She was so very angry. She's made up her mind, and won't listen to me. Maybe if Maeve were here ...'

'You don't need Maeve,' said Nellie. 'Oh, Lily, you are so brave and strong and clever – you can make this right all on your own.'

'I can't,' I said. 'It's too big for me to fix.'

'I could go with you,' said Nellie.

'No,' I said sadly. 'Thank you, but that won't help.'

I didn't know if it would help or not, but I couldn't let Nellie do anything that might put her own job in danger. She had no mam to take her in, and if she were sent away from Lissadell she might end up back in the workhouse.

'It's hopeless,' I said. 'There's nothing anyone can do.'

Now my friends held me close and hugged me again. They didn't speak – maybe because there were no more words to say.

* * *

I barely slept that night. I kept thinking what Mam would say when I told her I'd lost my good job at Lissadell. Even if she believed that none of it was my fault, that wouldn't change things. My family would never have anything nice again. We'd be close to starving. Would Denis have to leave school and

go to work? Maybe Jimmy too? What was going to become of us all?

Sometimes I thought of Maeve. This was her fault. If only she hadn't had the notion of going to Dublin, my life would be going on as normal. I'd be working away, waiting for Miss O'Brien to get married, and then moving on to my exciting new life as a teacher.

But then I remembered Maeve's sad face as she begged her mother to let her stay in Sligo. She was so terrified of going to boarding school, she didn't stop to think how things might turn out. She didn't mean to cause any trouble for me, and anyway, blaming her wasn't going to help me in the slightest. The damage was done, and nothing could change that now.

Once again I thought how little power we servants had. We depended on families like the Gore-Booths. We were all afraid of losing our jobs and our homes.

I remembered Sam's words. Was the world really going to change?

Would there be a time when girls like me could be

and do anything we wanted?

Was there a future where girls like me could wear trousers and go to university and drive motor cars and vote?

Maybe there was – but my future was right now, and it wasn't looking good.

Chapter Twenty-One

On Thursday morning I followed Nellie around the house like a girl in the middle of a bad dream. When the family had gone down to breakfast, Nellie and I went to clean their bedrooms.

'At least we don't have to do Lady Mary's room today,' she said brightly as we went up the servants' stairs. 'She's gone to visit her sister who's sick – and one less room is always a good thing, don't you think?'

I know Nellie was trying to cheer me up, but when she mentioned Lady Mary, I could feel tears rushing to my eyes again. All I'd ever got from that lady was fairness and generosity. She'd bought me the nicest Christmas presents I'd ever received. She'd given me many yards of the finest fabric to make clothes for Mam and my sisters. What was she going to say when she got back and heard that Mrs Bailey had sent me

home in disgrace? Would she be sad? Angry? Disappointed? Or would she soon get used to another housemaid, and forget that I'd ever existed?

'Lily?'

'What?' For a moment I'd forgotten where I was.

'I asked you a question,' said Nellie. 'Don't you think it's nice to have one room less to do?'

I looked at her sadly. I was going to miss her so much. Soon she'd be sharing our room with a new maid. Would that girl be her best friend? Would she sing that girl to sleep with her beautiful, sweet voice?

'I'm sorry, Nellie,' I said. 'I'm not in the mood for chatting this morning. Do you mind?'

She looked so sad and hurt I wanted to grab the words back, but how could I? I'd spoken the truth. My heart was breaking, and Nellie's gentle chatter couldn't change that.

* * *

After dinner, Cook called me into the kitchen.

'I've got a job for you, Lily,' she said.

'I'll go and get started on the nursery,' said Nellie, hurrying off. Usually we liked to work together, but maybe she was relieved to be getting away from me and my sadness. Maybe she was already planning a working life without me in it.

Cook was sitting at the big kitchen table. 'Here, love,' she said, patting the bench beside her. 'Sit down with me for a bit.'

When I sat beside her she put her arm around me. She smelled of flour and sugar and soap.

'The night you went missing was the worst,' she said. 'We were terribly worried about you – and when we heard you were safe in Dublin with Miss Maeve, we were so relieved – I have to tell you there were tears in many eyes around here.'

'I'm sorry you were all worried about us,' I said.

'Ah, sure we'll get over it. I don't know the half of what happened that day, but I do know you're a good

girl, and you don't deserve this.'

I felt a sudden rush of hope. Why hadn't I thought of this before? Maybe Cook could talk to Mrs Bailey. Maybe she could make things right again.

But Cook shook her head, as if she could read my thoughts. 'I'm sorry, love,' she said. 'I can't help you. I can't take Mrs Bailey on. This job is all I have, and if I lose it ...'

'I understand,' I said. 'I don't want anyone else getting into trouble.'

'I know your family enjoy the treats I've sent them, so I'll get Albert to bring a basket over whenever he can. I'll remember to send big slices of that chocolate cake they love so much – and a few custard tarts for you.'

'Oh, Cook, that's so kind.'

'Ah now,' she said, patting my hand. ''Tis a thing of nothing. I'd do more if I could.'

In the hallway I could hear a bell ringing. 'I'd better go,' I said.

'Let someone else go this time,' said Cook. 'Why don't you run out to the kitchen garden and get me some ... some ... now what is it I need again?'

I smiled, knowing Cook was only making an excuse. She knows how I love the few minutes outside in the fresh air.

'Some leeks!' she said. 'I think there's a few left and you can fetch me three or four.'

'I'm going to miss you so much,' I said, throwing my arms around her.

'And I'll miss you too,' she said, taking a hanky from her apron pocket and dabbing her eyes with it. 'Now off you go – and take your time – if anyone comes looking for you I'll tell them you're doing an important job for me.'

So I fetched the vegetable basket and ran outside.

* * *

The gardener dug up four fat leeks and shook them

free of earth, before placing them in my basket. I thanked him, and set off back to the house – taking the roundabout way, past the stables.

I walked slowly, listening to the scuffling sound my boots made on the gravel. I wondered if I'd ever again walk these familiar paths, if I'd ever again be allowed into such a fine and beautiful house.

I stopped when I heard a whistle, and then a voice calling my name.

'Lily! Wait for me.'

I stopped and let Sam catch up.

'Lily!' he said as came close. 'I can't believe you were in Dublin. It must have been such an adventure.'

'It was,' I said. 'But now ...'

Before I could finish, he took my hands in his, pulled me on to the soft grass, and began to dance around. 'Oh, we are such lucky people, you and me,' he said. 'You've had an adventure in Dublin, and soon I'll be off to join my fellow soldiers. Sligo isn't big enough for the lives we two are going to have.'

I pulled my hands away, but Sam was so happy and excited he didn't seem to notice. Clearly, though he'd heard about my trip to Dublin, he didn't know that, because of it, I was losing my job.

'Tell me all about Dublin,' he said. 'Was it very big? Was it noisy? What was the best thing you saw? Would you like to live there one day? Would you ...?'

Suddenly I didn't want to tell Sam I was leaving Lissadell. I didn't want to tell him how my life was about to change – and not in a good way.

'Let's talk about Dublin some other time,' I said. 'What happened here while I was away?'

'Well, the big news is that my papers arrived here yesterday,' he said. 'I had to tell Teddy my secret, because you weren't here, and I needed someone to read the letter for me.'

'And?'

'I'll be leaving next week – army life is the best, I know it is. Aren't you happy for me?'

'Oh, Sam!' I said shaking my head. 'No, I'm not

happy at all.'

The smile faded from his face. 'I'm your friend. If I'm happy, you should be happy.'

'But it's a war.'

'Exactly! You can read, Lily. You've seen the news-papers. We have to defend Belgium.'

'But you're only a …' I was going to say he was only a boy, but stopped, not wanting to hurt his feelings. 'You're not old enough yet,' I continued. 'You know you need to be eighteen to join up – and they make that rule for a reason.'

'By the time I'm eighteen, the war will be over, and it'll be too late for me to help.'

'I hope you're right,' I said. 'And until then, instead of fighting, maybe there's other things you could do to help the war effort.'

'Like what?'

All I could think of was knitting socks and vests, and somehow I couldn't imagine Sam doing that. 'I'm not sure,' I said. 'But leave it with me and I'll

think of something.'

'You won't have to, because I'll be ...'

Before he could say 'gone,' I heard Teddy calling. 'Sam – where are you? I need you here in the stables – now!'

'Got to go,' said Sam.

A horrible thought struck me. 'I might not see you again before ...'

'I'll see you lots,' he said with a grin. 'I'm not going until Thursday next week.'

'But tomorrow is my last ...' I stopped.

Could I tell him?

How could I say goodbye to my friend, knowing where he was going, and what might happen to him.

'Sam!' called Teddy again. 'Where have you got to?'

'Your last what?' asked Sam.

'Oh, nothing,' I said, trying to sound casual. 'Just ... Sam ... be careful ... don't take any stupid chances. Think of your mam and daddy ... don't ...'

He laughed and then started to run towards Ted-

dy's voice, calling over his shoulder to me as he went. 'I'm only going to the stables,' he said. 'And don't you worry, Lily, nothing's ever going to happen to me, I'm teak tough.'

I hurried back to the kitchen, not even trying to stop the tears that were flowing down my cheeks.

Chapter Twenty-Two

Friday was dark and dreary, suiting the way I felt.

Once again, I followed Nellie around the house, doing our endless work. As we finished each job, I thought – that's it – I'll never do that job again. And that made me sad, even though I'd hated most of the stupid boring tasks.

As I worked, I felt sick inside. Next morning I'd have to leave forever. Next morning, I'd have to go home and tell Mam that from now on, I couldn't give her any money. From now on, things were going to be very bad for our little family. Since I wouldn't be coming back to Lissadell, I couldn't even take Maeve's bicycle home, the way I usually did. I'd have to walk all the way there, with every step taking me closer to breaking my poor mam's heart.

Sometimes, to buck myself up, I reminded myself that none of this was my fault.

Sometimes I wondered, if Maeve had told me the truth, would I have gone with her to Dublin anyway?

* * *

I felt a sudden pain in my chest as I walked past the cupboard under the attic stairs. That's where Lady Mary keeps fabric and threads and things like that. That's where she tells me to go, any time I want, to collect things to make clothes for Mam and my sisters. For a second I thought I should take some fabric now. The girls would love two bright new dresses, and it would give me something to do in the long weeks ahead. But how could I do that? I was in disgrace, and taking fabric would be wrong.

'Lily!'

Before I could turn, Maeve had run up behind me, grabbed my arm and pulled me into her bedroom.

'Maeve! Why are you here? What's going on? What …?' I stopped talking as I looked properly at my friend. She was breathless, as if she'd run a hundred miles. Her long, wavy hair was wild and uncombed. Her skirt was grubby and ripped on one side. On her cheek was a dark smudge of mud.

'What happened to you?' I said. 'Are you hurt?'

She looked at her grubby appearance in the glass over the fireplace and shrugged. 'I'm fine. Just a bit untidy. I borrowed one of Gaga's horses and rode here.'

'From Ardeevin? But that's miles and miles.'

'I know. The poor horse is very tired, but Teddy is taking care of him now.'

'But why?'

'Gaga told me you're being sent away from Lissadell. I didn't want to believe her, so I came to find out. It's not true – is it?'

I nodded sadly.

'That's terrible – but they'll give you a reference,

won't they? You'll still be able to teach when Miss O'Brien finally gets married?'

I shook my head again, my sadness helped a tiny little bit by the fact that Maeve remembered all the details I'd told her about my dream of teaching.

'That's not fair,' she said. 'None of this is your fault.'

I didn't answer. We both knew she was right. 'Anyway, I got you into this mess, so it's my job to get you out of it,' she said

'Thank you – but aren't you going to be in trouble for taking Gaga's horse and coming here like this?'

'Possibly.'

'But you promised your mother! When she hears about this, you might get sent away to England.'

For a moment, Maeve looked as if she might cry, but then she shook her head. 'I know that – but I had to take the chance. How could I sit in Ardeevin for the next two years, knowing how I'd ruined your life? Boarding school might be bad, but it couldn't be as bad as that.'

I wanted to hug my wild and loyal friend.

'Does Gaga know you're here?' I asked.

'I've learned my lesson about disappearing. I told her groom to tell her.'

I looked nervously out the window. 'So she could come here any minute and …?'

Maeve laughed. 'I asked the groom to give me a head start, so Gaga won't come searching for a while. By the time she gets here, everything will be sorted out.'

'But …'

She held her finger to her lips. 'Hush, Lily. Leave this with me. Come on.'

She grabbed my hand and pulled me out of the room. When she led the way to the servants' stairs, I pulled her back.

'Where are we going?' I asked. 'What's your plan?'

'We're going to Mrs Bailey. I'll explain everything to her, and get your job back.'

I laughed as I started to follow my friend, but then

stopped, as I remembered Nellie's words. *Lily, you are so brave and strong and clever – you can make this right all on your own.*

'Come on, Lily,' said Maeve. 'There's no time to waste. We have to get this sorted out.'

'Thank you for coming all this way to help me,' I said. 'That's one of the nicest things anyone has ever done for me, but ...'

'Lily?'

'I'm not the nervous little girl who came to Lissadell with no idea of what to do and how to do it. I'm older now, and before long I hope I'll be a teacher. Now it's time for me to learn how to stand on my own two feet.'

'If you're sure?' Maeve didn't look sure at all, and that made me hesitate. How easy it would be to hide behind her, and let her try to make things right for me. But how could I go through life, always waiting for someone else to solve my problems? How could I teach little children to do the right thing, if I was too

afraid to do it myself?

I laughed. 'I think I'm sure, so I'm going to do it now before I change my mind.'

Maeve hugged me. 'I'll be right here, waiting for the good news.'

* * *

I stood outside the familiar black door, trying to breathe slowly, trying to ignore how my hands were shaking.

'Come.'

I opened the door and stepped inside. Mrs Bailey looked up from her notebook, but her face was blank, and I couldn't tell what she was thinking.

'Yes, Lily?'

She still had the cold, quiet voice. I wanted to turn and run away, but I knew that wasn't a good idea. I was only going to have one chance to make things right, and this was it. I closed the door and stood in

front of Mrs Bailey's desk.

'I am very, very sorry about that journey to Dublin, Mrs Bailey, but could you please allow me to explain exactly what happened?'

'I'm all ears,' she said, putting down her pen and folding her arms.

I took a deep breath and began my story. 'You see, when Maeve and I left Lady Mary in Sligo Town, I really truly thought we were only going for lunch and maybe a walk. But then Maeve brought us to the station, and ...'

Mrs Bailey didn't interrupt once while I told my story. A few times her eyes opened wide, but she didn't say a word.

'... and that's the full truth of what happened,' I said as I got to the end. 'By the time I realised what was going on, all I could do was support Maeve, and help her talk to her mother.'

For a long time, Mrs Bailey didn't say anything. She stared at me, tapping her fingers gently on the

desk. Did she believe me? Did she think I'd made up this story to get myself out of trouble?

'I was wrong about you, Lily,' she said in the end.

I was confused. Did she mean she was wrong when she thought I was a good girl, or when she thought I was a bad one? I held my breath and waited for her to continue.

'You're a fine, decent young girl, and we're lucky to have you at Lissadell.'

'So you believe me? You really believe me?'

For the first time, she smiled. 'Knowing you, and knowing Miss Maeve, that story makes perfect sense.'

'So?'

She put up her hand to stop me. 'Now let me explain for a moment. Before we knew where you were that evening, the whole house was in turmoil. I was so frightened for you and Miss Maeve; I swear it took ten years off my life. If anything had happened to you two girls, I'd have ... Anyway, you came back safely, and I should have known that *you* wouldn't

have done that to us. I've seen you do a hundred kind things every day and I know you wouldn't upset us like that. I was wrong to tell you to leave. I was wrong to say you don't deserve a reference. I hope you'll be with us for a while yet, but when the time comes, you shall have the finest reference ever written.'

My legs felt weak, and I held onto a chair so I wouldn't fall to the floor. 'So I can stay? I can really stay?'

Mrs Bailey laughed. 'Yes, Lily. Please stay as long as you like.'

'Thank you,' I said. 'Thank you so much.'

I was turning to go when there was a knock on the door, and a voice from the hallway.

'Mrs Bailey? Are you in there? I'd like to have a word.'

It was Lady Mary!

Chapter Twenty-Three

Mrs Bailey nodded at me and I opened the door. Lady Mary was still wearing her travelling coat, and a fine hat made of satin and lace. Maeve was standing next to her, still looking very grubby and untidy. They stepped into the office (which was now getting crowded), and Maeve whispered to me. 'I've told Aunt Mary everything. I said you want to sort it out on your own, but she insisted on coming down here to help you.'

I was glad I'd spoken up for myself, but it was nice to know that Lady Mary was on my side too.

'It's all fine,' I whispered back. 'I'm staying.'

Maeve squeezed my hand tightly. 'Oh, Lily, that's the best news I've ever heard.'

'Lady Mary – you're back!' said Mrs Bailey. 'Is your sister better?'

'She is perfectly well, thank you,' said Lady Mary. 'I think she was making rather a fuss about nothing. Now what is it I hear about Lily leaving us?'

Mrs Bailey looked uncomfortable. 'That has all been sorted out, Lady Mary,' she said. 'Lily isn't going anywhere for the moment.'

'But why on earth was such a thing even thought of? Lily has been a fine housemaid since the day she arrived here.'

Now I felt sorry for Mrs Bailey, but I was afraid if I said anything, I'd make things even worse for her.

'Allow me to explain, Lady Mary,' said Mrs Bailey. 'You departed in a hurry, and I didn't know when you'd be back. You left me in charge – so I had to make a decision.'

'Indeed,' said Lady Mary. A single word, which didn't tell us very much. Her face was blank, and I had no idea what she could have been thinking.

'I told Lily she had to go,' said Mrs Bailey. 'I didn't know the full story, and I'm afraid I wasn't prepared

to listen – but I realise now that I was wrong. I am sorry, Lady Mary. I am sorry, Lily.'

Now I had a new respect for the housekeeper. It was brave of her to say those words in front of Lady Mary and Maeve and me. Mam always says that when you make a mistake you should own up, and learn from it, but most people don't do that.

'You see, Lady Mary,' continued Mrs Bailey. 'I feel responsible for what happened.'

'How could you think any of this was your fault?' said Lady Mary. 'You weren't even in Sligo Town with us. How could you possibly have known what was going to happen?'

'Because ...' Mrs Bailey's face was pale, and she spoke in a big tumble of words. 'Because for the last year or more, I'm the one who released Lily from her work, so she could go running around the place with Miss Maeve. I know Lily should have been attending to her duties with the other servants, but I let myself be carried away by the girls' joy and sense of fun. I let

them think they could do anything they liked and, because of that, I caused great upset to everyone who lives in this lovely house. I didn't do my duty, and now it has come to this. It is my fault – all of it.'

At last I realised what was going on. Just like the rest of us, Mrs Bailey was scared of losing her job and her home and her future. I'd often heard her say that she was saving every penny of her wages so she and her sister and brother could buy a tiny cottage when they retire. That was her dream, and if she lost her job, her dream would also disappear.

'Mrs Bailey,' said Lady Mary, but Mrs Bailey interrupted her.

'If you could see past my bad judgement, Lady Mary, just this one time, I promise that in the future I will be more careful. I will keep the servants in check. If I lose this job, I will ...'

Lady Mary patted Mrs Bailey's arm. 'You are the best housekeeper in all the county,' she said. 'My friends are jealous that I'm lucky enough to have you

taking care of my home.'

Mrs Bailey looked confused. 'But Miss Maeve, and Lily ...'

Now Lady Mary put her arm around Maeve. 'Our little Maeve is lonely sometimes,' she said. 'She misses her mother and father. She has no friends of her own age here at Lissadell, and that is not right for a young girl.'

'But I allowed them to ...'

'I have always known of Maeve and Lily's little jaunts, Mrs Bailey,' said Lady Mary. 'And I fully approve. If I weren't happy, I would have let you know at once. You have done an excellent job of making sure that Lily spends time with my niece, while also attending satisfactorily to her duties. I don't know how you manage to run this house so well, I really don't.'

I watched as the fear slipped away from the house-keeper's face, and was replaced with a huge, glowing smile.

Now Lady Mary looked at Maeve. 'As for you, young lady, your grandmother is responsible for you while you're in Sligo. You will have to answer to her for your foolish and reckless behaviour.'

'I already have,' said Maeve. 'Extra lessons. No treats. Early to bed – my life will be a misery for weeks.'

I wanted to laugh when I looked at Maeve's face, which wasn't miserable at all. She looked delighted with the way things were turning out. Only then I remembered something – Maeve had promised her mother she'd behave. Surely slipping out of Ardeevin and coming all the way to Lissadell on a borrowed horse wouldn't count as good behaviour? Maeve said that being sent to boarding school was a price she was ready to pay to save me from losing my job, and my chance of being a teacher, but ...

'Lady Mary,' I said quickly. 'I know Maeve shouldn't really be here at Lissadell. She should be at Ardeevin doing her extra lessons – but she came here to help

me. She's kind and good and brave and loyal. Please don't let her be punished for that. Please don't ...'

'You two girls!' said Lady Mary. 'Always looking out for each other. Don't worry, I will have a word with Lady Gore-Booth, and I'm sure that on this occasion – and on this occasion only! – she can be persuaded to overlook what has happened.'

'Oh, thank you,' said Maeve running into her aunt's arms. I wanted to do the same, but knew that wasn't a good idea.

'Thank you,' Lady Mary,' I said. 'Thank you – for everything.'

Then a bell rang in the hallway, and I remembered who I was and where I was.

'That might be Sir Josslyn,' I said. 'I'd better go and see what he wants.'

So I straightened my cap, fixed my apron, and ran upstairs to do my work.

* * *

Five minutes later I found Nellie in the China room. She was busy, and didn't hear me coming in.

'You were right!' I said running towards her. 'I *was* able to speak up for myself. I explained everything to Mrs Bailey and I'm staying at Lissadell. I'm not in disgrace anymore.'

Careful Nellie put down the china teapot she was dusting, and turned to hug me.

'Lily!' she said. 'Oh, Lily, that's the very, very best news.'

Then my gentle, quiet friend took my hand and led the way through the servants' quarters, calling 'Lily's staying, Lily's staying,' to everyone we met.

* * *

That evening after tea, Nellie came and pulled me by the hand, hurrying me along the corridor.

'You're in a big rush to get back to work,' I said.

She laughed. 'I know there's a lot to do, but first

come outside to the kitchen courtyard. Johanna has a surprise for us.'

'Harry!' I said. 'Is Harry back?' But Nellie had run ahead, and didn't answer me.

Outside, Harry and Johanna were sitting on the edge of the little stone pond, holding hands and looking very sweet. Johanna was gazing at Harry as if he were the most beautiful person she'd ever seen. At first, I was confused. It looked as if Harry's injuries had disappeared. The cheek that used to be so badly injured now looked pink and smooth. Was this a miracle? Then, as I got closer, Harry lifted his head, and I could see the truth. He was wearing shiny new glasses, with dark lenses, so I couldn't see his injured eye. On one side, attached to the bottom frame of the glasses, was a piece of smooth pink plastic, like a mask. He had grown a thick moustache, so I couldn't see for sure where the mask ended.

'Hello, Harry,' I said, not trusting myself to say any more.

'Girls!' said Harry, jumping up and turning his face from side to side. 'What do you think of my mask?'

I didn't know what to say. It was true, the mask hid his bad eye, and his scars, but it also hid Harry, the man I knew and loved. It was like looking at a stranger.

'Harry!' said Nellie, hurrying over and giving him a sisterly hug. 'I don't think you needed a mask at all – you were perfect the way you were. But as for masks, I'm sure that is the finest one in the whole world – though I can't say I've seen very many.'

Now we all laughed, and Harry's uninjured eye crinkled up, and once again I could see the man I remembered, and everything was fine again.

'Are you back for good, Harry?' I asked. 'Will you be starting work again?'

'I'm fit and well,' he said. 'But Sir Josslyn said I can stay at home with my parents for another few days. I'll be back annoying you all next week though, so be prepared.'

'Johanna will be the happiest girl in Ireland then,' I teased, poking her in the ribs.

'Oh, I won't have to wait till next week,' smiled Johanna, gazing at Harry as if she could hardly believe he were there in front of us. 'On my day off I'm going to visit him in his parents' house. It's not far at all – and they are going to make tea for me and everything.'

Nellie and I looked at each other grinning. Harry's parents would have to love Johanna – and if they were inviting her to tea, then it meant that her relationship with Harry must be very serious.

'Lily! Nellie! Where have you two girls got to now?'

'Mrs Bailey!' said Nellie. 'We have to go.'

'Bye, Harry. See you next week, Harry,' we called as we ran inside.

And all evening, I could hardly concentrate on my work as I wondered if it was too soon to start thinking about making a wedding dress for my friend.

Chapter Twenty-Four

Next morning, I went to the coach house to collect Maeve's bicycle for the journey home. As I cycled along the big driveway, I felt happy and light and free. All was well. My job and my reference were safe. I wouldn't have to tell Mam.

Then a heard a familiar voice. 'Hello, Lily!' And I remembered there were more troubles in the world than the ones I had.

I stopped and turned to face Sam, who was leading one of Sir Josslyn's horses along a grassy path out of the woods.

'Poor girl,' he said, patting the horse's neck. 'One of her back feet is lame. Teddy's going to show me how to make a poultice to bring down the swelling.'

'You love the horses, don't you?' I said, watching how gentle he was.

'I sure do. I'm hoping that if I do well in the army, maybe I could change to the cavalry. Then I could be with the horses all day long.'

'But it wouldn't be like this!' I said, thinking of the newspaper reports I'd read. 'It wouldn't be lovely quiet woods and fields. In the war there'll be guns and tanks and mud and cold. The horses will be afraid all the time. *You* will be afraid all the time.'

'Sure, I'm hardy,' said Sam with a big grin. 'I'm afraid of nothing at all.'

'But what about the horses?' I said, thinking this might help my argument. 'Wouldn't you hate to see them cold and hungry and frightened?'

'I *would* hate that,' he said. 'But at least if I were there, I could help them, and calm them down a bit.'

'Oh, Sam,' I said, wanting to shake him. 'By the time you realise how wrong you are about all of this, you'll be stuck in a filthy trench out there, and it will be much, much too late.'

'You're a girl, Lily,' he said. 'You wouldn't under-

stand.'

Now I wanted to shake him *and* punch him, but he gave a big laugh. 'I'm only teasing you, is all,' he said. 'Now I'd better look after this girl, before the swelling gets worse. See you soon.'

He led the horse away and I continued my journey, sadder than before.

* * *

Mam was tending the small flower bed in front of our house. I propped the bicycle against the wall, then ran and hugged her as if I never wanted to let go. I breathed in the familiar smells of warmth and comfort and home.

'My little pet,' she said, over and over again, stroking my hair. 'My dear little pet.'

In the end I released her, and followed her inside to the warmth of our little house. The children were off playing or working somewhere, and I was glad to

have Mam to myself for once.

I sat on the little stone ledge by the fire, while Mam heated some milk. Then she handed me the steaming mug and sat on the ledge opposite.

'Tell Mam everything,' she said.

And then, even though I'd decided not to worry her, I told her every single thing about my friendship with Maeve, my trip to Dublin, and what happened afterwards. When I finished, Mam didn't say anything for a long time.

'Mam?' I said. 'Are you very cross with me?'

'My girl,' she said. 'Why on earth would I be cross?'

'Because I've been friends with Maeve de Marki-evicz for ages, and you never even knew?'

'Ah, child, don't you know how small Sligo is? People have little else to do but gossip.'

'So you knew all the time?'

She nodded. 'I've known a fair while all right. I understood you'd tell me about it in your own good time.'

'And you weren't cross about our friendship?'

'The way I heard it told, that Markievicz girl is a sad little thing – and you've been kind to her, the way Daddy and I always taught you to be.'

'But ...'

'Lily, you're a grown girl now. I trust you to do the right thing.'

'And the trip to Dublin?'

'Well, there was some talk about that too – though I'm glad that by the time I heard, you were already back at Lissadell. If the Gore-Booths had come here and told me you were missing, I'd surely have lost my mind for fretting.'

'What kind of talk was there?'

'I'm afraid it wasn't all very good. Some people are idle, and some are jealous, and some simply aren't very nice.'

'Oh, Mam. Did you think badly of me when you heard the stories?'

'Never, my girl. I knew there would be a good

explanation, and sure wasn't I right?'

'Do you think the Master might have heard?'

'I'd say he very likely did. There's not much happens around here that he doesn't know about.'

'So maybe he'll think I wouldn't be a good person to be teaching the children at his school? I'll have my good reference, but what if the Master chooses to ignore it?'

'That definitely won't happen, my pet.'

'How can you be so sure?'

She smiled. 'Because The Master has known you since you were tiny, just like I have. He knows you're a steady, honest soul. And besides, I met him this morning, and he told me how he's looking forward to having you work with him, as soon as Miss O'Brien moves away.'

'He really said that?'

She patted my knee. 'Yes, darling. He really did.

'Oh Mam,' I sighed. 'I don't want to let you or the Master down. I hope I'm as good as you both

think I am.'

'I know how good you are,' she said gently. 'But if you're not sure yourself, then answer one question for me.'

'What?'

'If Maeve had told you the plan for a secret trip to Dublin, would you have gone along with it?'

When Mam stares at me in a particular way, telling the truth is the only option – but what was the truth? Would I really have helped Maeve if she'd been honest with me? I didn't answer for a long time as I ran all the details through my head – how sad Maeve felt, what a mad idea it was, how angry Gaga was, how afraid Mam would have been if she'd known. And finally, when my head hurt from thinking, I knew the answer.

'No, Mam,' I said. 'If I had known, I wouldn't have gone with Maeve. I'd have tried to help her some other way, but I wouldn't have gone to Dublin without anyone knowing. I wouldn't risk hurting you or

anyone else.'

'That's my dear girl,' said Mam, leaning over to pat my hand. 'And Maeve knew too, that's why she didn't tell you what she planned to do. I'm sure she's a good girl, but she's not as good as you.'

I smiled at Mam. It was such a relief that she knew about Maeve, and how my life really was at Lissadell. Mam had barely ever left this little village, and I wondered how she became so wise. Did she have the answers to every problem in the world? And then I remembered.

'Mam,' I said. 'If you make a promise, but keeping it means that someone might get hurt, or even killed, what should you do?'

'I think you need to tell me a little bit more,' she said.

'There's this boy I know, called Sam ...'

* * *

I was crying by the time I'd finished telling Mam about Sam, and she had tears in her eyes too.

'Ah, the poor boy,' she said. 'It sounds as if he has no idea what he's getting himself into.'

'You're right – but what should I do? Should I try and find where his parents live, and go and tell them? Should I tell the Gore-Booths? Oh, Mam, I'd hate to be a tell-tale, but if telling tales could save Sam's life ...'

Mam leaned over and patted my knee. 'Sometimes breaking a promise is the right thing to do,' she said. 'But in this case, I don't think telling on your friend will make any difference. If he's determined to go, he'll find a way in the end – no matter what you do. I've heard terrible stories of young boys touring the towns of Ireland until they find a recruiting officer who'll believe their lies. I heard that in Donegal a boy of twelve managed to sign up. What were they thinking of at all – the lad was barely out of nappies!'

'So there's nothing I can do?'

'That's not what I'm saying at all, at all. What I'm saying is, as long as Sam believes going to war is the right thing for him to do, then he'll do it. You've got to make him change his mind about the whole idea.'

'But Mam – I've tried so much. I've talked to him, and begged him, over and over again. He's as stubborn as Carty's old donkey.'

'Tell me this, Lily, when you're above in the school teaching the big girls how to knit, will you stand at the blackboard and write down words to explain how to do the stitches?'

'Mam! Sam's life is at stake. Why are you talking about knitting?'

'You'll see – now answer my question.'

'Of course I won't stand at the blackboard to teach knitting – the girls would never learn that way. I'll sit down beside them with my needles and wool and show them what to do.'

Mam smiled. 'Of course – everyone understands better when they're shown things.'

'But fighting isn't the same as knitting! I can't take Sam out to Belgium and *show* him what war is like, and then get back home in time for dinner.'

'Now, Miss, no need for that cheeky talk.'

'Sorry, Mam.'

'If you have a little think, maybe something will come to you.'

For a second I felt cross. This was important, so why was Mam talking in riddles? But she was sitting there, warming her hands by the fire, all calm and serious, and she'd never once put me wrong in my whole life, so I closed my eyes, and thought and thought and thought and ...

'Harry!'

'Is that the name of your friend who was wounded in the war?'

'Yes. Oh, Mam, you are so clever. If Sam talks to Harry and sees his injuries, then he'll understand what war is really like. He'll understand why he should wait until he's eighteen to sign up.'

'And can you arrange that meeting in time?'

'I think so. Probably if I ...'

'Lily!' I couldn't say any more as my brothers and sisters rushed into the room, and my sisters jumped on me, and my brothers jumped on Cook's basket and my darling little home was full of merriment and fun and laughter.

Chapter Twenty-Five

'I'm really not meant to be here,' said Sam, reluctantly following me along the path to the kitchen garden. 'I should be cleaning out the stables. I know I'm leaving for the army in a few days, but I'd prefer not to get into trouble before then. Teddy can be fair cross when you get on the wrong side of him.'

I wanted to slap him. I'd had to skip dinner so I could cycle to Harry's house and tell him the plan, and then I had to persuade Mrs Bailey to let me out of work for an hour. Did Sam have any idea of the trouble I'd gone to? Did he have any idea how important it was to me that this plan would work?

'Just come along,' I said. 'I'm not meant to be here either, but there's someone I want you to meet. I've told him ... well I've told him all about you and the army.'

'But you promised not to tell anyone.'

'I know, and I'm sorry, but Harry is a soldier and ...'

'Oh, an army man like me. That's all right then,' said Sam in a voice that was deeper than usual. I didn't know whether to laugh or cry. I could tell he was trying to sound older than his age, but it wasn't working. He sounded like my little brothers – only pretending to be grown up.

I pushed open the little gate that led into the kitchen garden, and was glad to see that, as planned, Harry was sitting on the bench by the water trough.

'Sam,' I said. 'This is my friend Harry. Harry, this is my friend, Sam.'

Harry stood up and they shook hands. Harry was wearing his new mask, but if Sam thought this was strange, he didn't show it.

'Hello, Sam,' said Harry. 'I know you're not eighteen yet, but I hear you've signed up for the army.'

'I have,' said Sam in his new deep voice. 'I can't wait until I'm eighteen. I'm in a hurry to get there

and show the enemy I mean business. It will be such a big adventure.'

'It's not exactly an adventure,' said Harry. 'War is wet and cold and loud and terrifying.'

'I'm not afraid of hardship,' said Sam. 'I'm ready for whatever happens.'

Harry looked at me, and when I nodded, he removed his glasses and mask, and turned to face Sam again. 'This is what happened to me,' he said. 'And after some of the things I've seen in battle, I consider myself a lucky man.'

Sam's gaze didn't falter, but I could see the colour draining from his cheeks. Then he gave a brave smile as he pushed out his chest, and tried to look taller than he was.

'I'm sorry that happened to you, Harry, but it won't change my mind about going to war. I'm strong enough to fight so it would be selfish to let fear keep me away.'

Why wasn't this working? I'd thought that one

look at Harry's face would make Sam change his mind. Clearly he was tougher than I'd realised.

'Harry is being brave, Sam,' I said desperately. 'But what happened to him is really bad. He will never see out of one of his eyes again, and those scars hurt all the time. His poor mother will probably never get over the shock of seeing him when he came home from the war. It's really very ...'

Harry put his hand on my arm, and shook his head to make me stop talking. I suppose he could see I was wasting my breath.

'You're a brave lad, Sam,' he said. 'And I can see that you think about others.'

'Of course I do,' said Sam. 'My mammy raised me to always think of the other person.'

'In that case,' said Harry. 'There's something you should know. I spent many months in battle, and met lots of young lads like you – lads who shouldn't have been in the army at all. Like you, they were strong and brave and determined.'

I glared at Harry. What was he doing? Had he forgotten he was supposed to be putting Sam off joining the army? But he gave me a little smile and continued.

'Those lads were doing their best, but in the end, they didn't help at all. They were more trouble than anything else.'

'But I wouldn't be ...' began Sam.

Harry cut him off. 'They lied about their age, but in fact, they weren't fooling anybody – and that was the trouble. They reminded the older soldiers of their sons and nephews and younger brothers. They felt they had to protect them, and look out for them, and that was a distraction for everybody. The truth is, the army would have been better off without those young lads.'

'But ...' Sam tried to interrupt, but once again, Harry didn't let him. When he continued, he sounded angry. His scars turned redder than before and his damaged eye began to twitch.

'When young boys like you go to war, everybody suffers, not only them. If you want to help your country, and the poor Belgians, then the best thing you can do is stay at home. Do you understand me, lad?'

Sam nodded slowly. I felt sorry for him as he looked like a little boy, in trouble with his daddy.

Harry continued, sounding gentler. 'In times of trouble we have to work together, and we all have different responsibilities. If this terrible war goes on until you are eighteen, it will be time enough then for you to fight. For now, your responsibility is to stay at home and work hard and get strong – so you'll be ready when you're needed.'

Sam put his head down. 'I only wanted to help,' he said in his normal voice, without a trace of that strange, fake deepness.

'I know you did, lad,' said Sam, patting him on the shoulder. 'I know you did.'

* * *

Sam kicked a stone along the path as we headed back to the house.

'I feel so stupid,' he said. 'Harry is a strong, brave man, and I'm just a ...'

'You're strong and brave too,' I said.

'But strong and brave isn't enough. It won't help anyone if I'm stuck here. Don't you understand? I want to be useful.'

'Nellie and I are still knitting socks for the soldiers,' I said. 'Maybe you could ...'

'Are you suggesting I sit around knitting socks?' he said, angrily kicking the stone into a shrub.

I was fairly sure Sam would hate knitting, but as I had no other ideas, that's exactly what I was going to suggest. His reaction changed my mind though.

'I wasn't going to say knitting,' I lied. 'I was just trying to think what you could do to help. There has to be something.'

'Like what?'

'I haven't worked it out yet – but I will – I promise.'

'Thanks, Lily,' he said. 'You're a good friend.'

I was glad to hear him say that, but also worried. What on earth *could* he do to help the war effort?

But now Sam seemed happy that he'd passed the problem on to me. He ran ahead, and I ran after him, stopping when we got to the place where we had to part.

As I turned to head for the house, Sam gave a big laugh. 'I really did want to fight,' he said. 'And I'm sorry it turned out like this, but at least there's one good thing.'

'What's that?'

'Now I won't have to face my mam and tell her what I did.'

I smiled. My friend was back.

Chapter Twenty-Six

ellie was standing outside Maeve's bedroom with a dreamy look on her face, like a girl in a trance. As I got closer, I could tell why. Maeve was practising her violin again.

'Oh, Lily,' sighed Nellie. 'I could stand here all the day long. That girl plays like a real, live angel.'

Nellie was right. I don't know very much about violin music, but even I could tell that Maeve was talented.

'She practises for hours every day,' said Nellie. 'She's going to be the star of the war concert. Sometimes I invent excuses so I can come up here and listen for a minute. Is that very bad of me?'

'Ah, Nellie,' I laughed. 'If that's the worst thing you ever do, then I think the Gore-Booths will have no complaint.'

We listened for a minute, and then went on with our cleaning. After the recent excitement, I was bored again. I didn't fancy another trip all the way to Dublin, but the occasional walk with Maeve across the fields, or to the beach would have been nice. I'd barely seen Maeve though, and when I did, she was always rushing back to her room for more violin practice. I missed my friend and the fun we used to have together.

'Hello, girls.' I didn't have to turn to tell that it was Lady Mary who'd come up behind us. I'd know that sweet voice anywhere.

'Will either of you be taking part in the war concert?' she asked.

'Not me,' I said quickly. 'My best talent is sewing, and I don't think that would be very interesting for people to watch.'

'And what about you, Nellie?' asked Lady Mary. 'I believe you have a beautiful singing voice.'

Nellie's face turned pink. 'Oh no, Lady Mary,' she

said. 'Sometimes I like to sing for Lily and Johanna, but no one would want to listen to me at a concert. I'm not good enough for that.'

Poor Nellie. After all her years in the workhouse, she had no confidence in herself at all. She never realised how good she was at so many things. Maybe if she sang in the concert and people loved her, that would make her feel better about herself.

'But you're the best singer I've ever heard,' I said. 'You should join in the concert. You should …'

I had lots more to say, but stopped talking as the pink faded from Nellie's cheeks and she became deathly pale. I could see that my friend was terrified.

When Lady Mary began to walk away, I turned to Nellie. 'I wish you'd try the concert,' I said. 'You could sing one very short and easy song. Everyone would love you, and maybe after that you'd be brave enough to try other things you never dared before. Entering the concert could change your life.'

She laughed, and I was glad to see the colour

coming back to her cheeks. 'Oh, Lily,' she said. 'Don't you understand? I don't want to change my life. It's simply perfect as it is.'

Lady Mary was about to go into her bedroom when I thought of something else.

'Lady Mary,' I said running over to her. 'About the concert.'

'Have you changed your mind, Lily?' she asked. 'Have you another wonderful talent I don't know about?'

'No, it's not me. It's Sam from the stables. Do you think he could help in the preparations for the concert? He's good at making things, so maybe he could help to build the stage or the backgrounds or something? He really, really wants to help with the war effort.'

'That's good of him, but I'm afraid there's no need. Sir Josslyn is in charge of building and construction, and he tells me everything is under control. For the past few days he's been turning volunteers away.

Young Sam will have to find another way to support our soldiers.'

* * *

Soon all anyone could talk about was the concert. For the first time ever, servants and family worked together as if they were equals. Maeve was playing violin of course, and Gaga planned to accompany her on the piano. Some of Lady Mary and Sir Josslyn's friends were putting together a choir. Ita and Delia planned to do a comedy sketch, and Isabelle was going to recite a poem. Cook planned to make hundreds of cakes and pastries to sell to the audience in the interval. Every time I stepped outside the house, all I could hear was hammering and sawing and the sound of men laughing and joking as they worked. War is a miserable business, but it was making people feel useful, which I suppose is a good thing.

One afternoon Cook asked me to bring some lem-

onade to the men working on the stage. As I made my way back to the kitchen, from behind a hedge, I heard a young man singing. It was so beautiful, I found myself tiptoeing over to hear better, thinking it was surely one of Sir Josslyn's friends practising for the choir.

I stopped at the end of the hedge, and listened. It was a sad love song, sung with such emotion, I could feel tears come to my eyes. It reminded me of Daddy and Mam, and how they used to hug, and sometimes dance together in our tiny little house. It made me sad and happy all at once.

When the song was over, without thinking, I clapped my hands loudly, hoping that whoever was there might sing another song. Then I heard a rustling and Sam appeared from behind the hedge, with one of Sir Josslyn's old dogs in his arms.

'Sam,' I said. 'Did you hear that beautiful singing? It truly brought a tear to my eye. I wonder who ...?'

He smiled and then I understood.

'That was you?'

'Yes.'

'You never told me you could sing like that.'

'You never asked.'

'But your voice is so lovely.'

He shrugged as if this were news to him. 'Is it?'

'Yes, it is. How come you don't know this? Didn't your teacher ever tell you?'

'Nah. At school only the girls liked singing. Any boy who showed an interest was teased and called soft. I liked to listen to the girls, and that's how I know the words, but I learned to never sing out loud.'

'Except for just now,' I said.

'Ah that was different. I was singing for poor Bessie,' he said, stroking the dog in his arms. 'She's sick, and I don't think she'll last more than a few days. She's in pain, so when I can, I bring her somewhere quiet, and sing to her. She seems to like it.'

'*Everyone* would like it,' I said. 'If they got a chance to hear it. Oh, Sam, would you sing in the concert at

all? It would be a way for you to help the war effort, and everyone would love you – I know they would.'

And it turned out that, unlike Nellie, Sam wasn't at all afraid of trying new things.

'Oh, all right then,' he said. 'I'll do it. Who should I talk to?'

So I spoke to Lady Mary, and soon everything was ready for Sam's first appearance on stage.

Chapter Twenty-Seven

The concert was on a Friday night, and all day long the estate was buzzing, with people running here and there putting last minute touches to the stage and the seating area, performers practising their concert pieces, and Cook going mad in the kitchen with the stress of all the extra work.

'Are you excited, Maeve?' I asked her when I met her on the stairs after breakfast.

'Very,' she said. 'I didn't love playing the violin before, but now it's one of my favourite things. When I go to boarding school, I think I might join a musical group there.'

I smiled. Now that Maeve didn't have to go to school for two years, the idea didn't scare her anymore. I knew that, when the time came, she'd be ready, and she'd do her very best to be happy there.

* * *

The Gore-Booths dined early that evening, and as soon as the tables were cleared, Nellie and I were allowed to go to the concert.

The tent was packed full, with most of the seats already taken.

'Lily! Over here. We've saved you a place.'

I turned to see Mam and my little brothers and sisters, all lined up in a row near the front. Lady Mary knew my family could never afford a shilling for each concert ticket, and had very kindly given me one for each of them. I ran over and hugged them all, and then sat on the seat they'd saved for me. I took Winnie onto my knee so there'd be room for Nellie too.

'I'm so excited,' said Nellie, looking about ready to faint away. 'I've never been to a concert before.'

'None of us has,' I said laughing. 'So, we don't know what to expect, but I'm sure it will be wonderful.'

And it was!

There were comedy acts, and poetry recitations and a juggler and singers and musicians and a man with a dog who could dance. Maeve was a star, and when she finished playing everyone stood up and clapped for ages. She bowed and looked delighted with herself, and Mam leaned over and patted my arm. 'Maeve seems like a lovely girl. You're lucky to have a friend like her.'

After that there was an unexpected drama when the curtain at the front of the stage came crashing down. Denis and Jimmy ran over to help, and when they came back, saying Sir Josslyn had given them a penny for being such fine men, they were so happy they were glowing.

The newly-fixed curtain went up slowly, and a bright light shone on the only person standing perfectly still in the centre of the stage. It took me a moment to recognise him, with his curls combed flat, and wearing a suit and a spotless white shirt. Then I laughed.

'It's Sam,' I said to Mam. 'The boy I told you about.'

On the platform in front of the stage, Lady Mary's friend began to play the piano, and a second later, Sam joined in. Nobody stirred as he sang a funny song, and then a happy one, and then a third, so sad that most of the audience couldn't hear it properly as they were busy pretending not to cry. When the clapping finally died down, I turned to Mam, who was dabbing her eyes with her best hanky.

'Oh dear,' she sighed. 'I don't know if I'm sad or happy or what. I feel as if I've been to heaven and back a few times in the last ten minutes. I only wish your daddy could have been here to enjoy it with us.'

Then she couldn't say any more, as Sam left the stage, and a group of dancers began a merry reel.

* * *

During the break, I bought some cakes for us to share, and Maeve came over with a jug of lemon-

ade and glasses. Mam told Maeve how she loved her music, and the two of them chatted easily, and that made me very happy.

Sam came over and everyone patted him on the back, and he laughed and said, 'sure I was only singing a few songs – but I've got a bit of a problem now.'

'What's that?' I asked.

'They want me to sing one more song right after the break – and there's been a special request for *When Irish Eyes are Smiling* – only I don't know all the words. I wonder could anyone help me?'

What was he doing? I'd told him many times that was Nellie's favourite song, and she often sang it while we were knitting. I stared at him, and he gave me a big wink, and I began to understand.

'I know all the words,' said Nellie. 'I could write them down for you if we could find a pencil and some ...' Before she could finish, the ushers began to call to everyone back to their seats for the second part of the concert.

'No time for writing,' said Sam. 'And anyway, I can't read.' (*Yet!* I thought, suddenly realising how I was going to spend my spare time over the coming weeks.)

'You'll have to help him, Nellie,' said Maeve.

'But I ...' began Nellie.

'If you don't help me, Nellie,' said Sam, with a mournful look on his face. 'I'll look like a right eejit up there and everyone will laugh at me.' And sweet, kind Nellie couldn't let that happen, so she let him lead her towards the stage.

When the curtain went up, Nellie and Sam stood together in the centre of the stage. (Though I don't know how Nellie was managing to stand, as she was shaking all over.)

The piano began to play and, as if they'd been practising all their lives, Nellie and Sam started to sing. Their voices went beautifully together, and after the first few lines, Nellie didn't look afraid anymore. She looked as if she were born to be on the stage.

When the song was over, everyone clapped and cheered like mad, and Sam held Nellie's hand as they bowed, and I smiled as her cheeks turned pink.

While the next act was getting ready, Nellie came back to her seat. 'You were the best!' I said. 'The best in the whole show.'

'You're a true star,' said Mam. 'And I'm sure your dear mam and dad would be very proud if they could see you now.'

'Thank you,' said Nellie, beaming.

'Maybe you could sing in another concert some time,' I said.

'No chance!' said Nellie. 'I did it this once, and I'm glad I did, but I'm never doing it again, and that's for certain sure.'

Now Sam came over. 'That was fantastic!' he said. 'Well done, Nellie.'

'Thank you,' she said. 'I ...' Then she stopped as she realised something everyone else had noticed already. 'You knew the words, Sam! You knew every single one.'

'They sort of came back to me once I got going,' he said, and we all laughed.

* * *

'I don't want to go home – ever,' said Denis, when the last act was over, and the curtain had once more come crashing to the ground, though this time no one bothered to fix it.

'It was the best night of my whole life,' sighed Jimmy.

The little girls said nothing, as they were curled up under the seats, fast asleep.

Mam and I said goodbye to Nellie, Maeve and Sam. Then we gathered my sisters into our arms and carried them to where Mam's neighbour was waiting with his pony and cart, ready to take them home again. Mam and I laid the girls on a rug, and the boys climbed up to their favourite spot on the bench next to the driver.

Mam hugged me and climbed up next to Winnie and Anne. 'See you tomorrow, my darling girl,' she said.

I laughed and climbed up beside her. 'Surprise!' I said. 'Mrs Bailey says I can come home with you tonight and sleep there and everything.'

And Mam hugged me again, because it was such a special treat for both of us; me spending a night with my family, at home, in the place in the world where I felt most safe and loved.

* * *

We carried the girls straight to bed, and the boys followed soon after, protesting that they weren't tired at all, though their eyes were red from yawning.

Mam and I sat by the fire, enjoying the precious quiet moments together. She will always be my mam, even when I'm an old, old lady, but in those still moments together, we were friends too. I told her all

about Sam's meeting with Harry, and how glad I was that her idea had worked.

'Lily, pet,' said Mam then. 'We need to have a word.'

'What?' something in her voice told me she wasn't going to be sharing good news with me.

'The Master called over today, just before we left for the concert. He said he'd like to talk to you, so he's coming back in the morning.'

Her words were making me very happy, so I managed to ignore the way her voice sounded. I felt all warm and excited. 'Oh, Mam, do you think Miss O'Brien is finally getting married? Maybe the Master's coming to tell me she's leaving, and I can start work as a Junior Assistant Mistress?'

Mam took a long moment to answer, but her serious face made me worried. 'The Master didn't say what he wants to talk to you about,' she said. 'But I don't think Miss O'Brien will be getting married any time soon.'

'How do you know?'

'I met Sally Clancy the other day – she's Miss O'Brien's aunt, you know.'

I didn't know that, and didn't care either. 'What did Sally say?'

'Oh, that woman goes on a bit, but the jist of it is that Miss O'Brien has all their hearts broken with her dithering. She's found herself a nice young man, but she won't agree to set a wedding date, and move to his home place in Donegal. She's getting on a bit, and if she lets that fella get away, she might not get another chance to marry.'

Suddenly I hated Miss O'Brien. She'd been teaching for years and years. Why couldn't she get on with it and move away and give *me* a chance?

Then I thought of something worse. 'If Miss O'Brien isn't leaving,' I said. 'Why did the Master want to talk to me?'

Mam didn't answer.

'Mam? Is there something you're not telling me?'

'Oh, Lily, I don't want to upset you, but ...'

'I'll know tomorrow anyway, Mam, so you might as well tell me.'

'The Master said he'd heard some disappointing news, and as a result, he needed to talk to you.'

Now I felt sick. 'It must be about my trip to Dublin with Maeve. He must have decided I'm not to be trusted.'

I wanted Mam to disagree with me, but she didn't. 'I don't know, pet,' she said, patting my hand with her warm strong one. 'I really don't know.'

'Oh, Mam!' I cried. 'Do you think the Master is coming to tell me to forget all about teaching in his school? Do you think he's coming to say that if Miss O'Brien ever gets her act together and moves to Donegal, he's going to give the job to someone else?'

'I'm not sure, my darling.'

Then I thought of something. There was a girl called Frances in the class below me at school. She was prissy and sweet and perfect – and always suck-ing up to the Master. Was he coming to tell me she

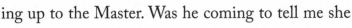

was going to be the new assistant when Miss O'Brien left? Was he coming to tell me that my dream was over forever?

'Ah now,' said Mam. 'Try not to fret. 'Tis time enough to worry about bad things when they actually happen. Now off you go to bed, and we'll see how things are in the morning.'

That night I should have slept like a baby. I was warm and safe in the bed with my brothers and sisters, and Mam close by. Maeve was happy because she had two more years at home at Lissadell. Sam was happy because he was the star of the concert. But I wasn't happy. I cried until the pillow I shared with Winnie was soaking wet from my tears.

Chapter Twenty-Eight

My days off were precious, but this one went much too slowly. The morning dragged as I waited for the knock on the door. I played with my little sisters, trying to let myself be distracted by the funny things they said and did. It didn't work though. All I could think of was the Master's visit, and what he was going to say.

* * *

'The Master is coming!' Denis ran in all excited to be the bearer of news. 'He's nearly here.'

Mam hugged me. 'Whatever he says, you're strong enough to take it, my girl. Remember that what's for you won't pass you by.'

I looked around the small room. When visi-

tors came to Lissadell there were so many rooms they could go to, but in our house there was only the kitchen and the tiny children's bedroom. Where could the Master and I even go to talk?

Mam pushed me towards the door. 'It's sunny enough to sit on the bench outside,' she said. 'I'll keep the children in here with me.'

When I got outside, the Master was already at the little gate. 'Lily!' he said. 'It's good to see you.'

'Hello, Sir,' I said, suddenly feeling shy. 'Would you like ... to sit here on our bench? Would you like a ... cup of water or milk?'

'Nothing for me, thank you.' He sat on the bench, and I sat beside him.

'I'll get straight to the point,' he said. 'I've come to talk to you about the position of Junior Assistant Mistress at the school.'

I wanted him to stop talking. I wanted to run inside to Mam and bury my head in her apron, and let her stroke my hair and make the world slip away. But I

was grown now, and couldn't hide from my troubles any more.

'Oh,' I said. 'Is this about me and Maeve de Markievicz? Because ...' I stopped talking. If the Master had made up his mind, who was I to try to change it?

'Yesterday I heard some very disappointing news,' he said. 'And it's going to change things for you, Lily.'

I wanted to block my ears, but stopped myself. I might not have hopes of being a teacher, but that didn't mean I had to act like a big baby.

'Miss O'Brien came to me after school yesterday and she was very upset.'

'Why?' I wondered if her man had got fed up of waiting, and decided not to marry her after all.

'Her fiancé has suddenly joined the army, and leaves for training in England next week.'

My heart sank even further than before. What if he was gone for years? What if he was killed?

Now the Master smiled. 'It seems this has finally knocked some sense into Miss O'Brien's head. She

announced that she's leaving Sligo this very morning. She is to be married on Monday, and when her husband departs, she will stay with his parents in Donegal until he comes back.'

'So she's really leaving Sligo?'

'She has very likely already left. We said our goodbyes yesterday, and I don't expect to see her again. It is inconvenient, but I suppose in times of war, we have to be understanding.'

'So that means …?'

'That means that from Monday, the school has a vacancy.'

'And?' It was a squeak more than a word.

'Will you be able to provide a good written reference from your employment at Lissadell House?'

'Yes! They promised.'

'Well in that case, Lily Brennan, I would like to offer you the position of Junior Assistant Mistress, starting a week from Monday. I presume that will be enough notice for your employers?'

I nodded, but couldn't say a single word. I held tightly to the bench, as otherwise I would surely have fallen to the ground.

'Lily?'

'I ... I ... I don't know what to say.'

'How about saying you would be delighted to accept the position?'

'I'd be delighted to accept the position,' I said. 'Thank you, Sir. Thank you so very much. I promise I won't let you down. I will be the best assistant the school has ever seen.'

The Master patted my shoulder as he stood up.

'I know you will be a big success,' he said. 'I will see you at nine o'clock on Monday week – and please bring the reference so I can pass it on to the education board, and they can do all the necessary paperwork from there.'

As he got to the front gate he turned. 'Oh, you were saying something about a jaunt with that girl of the Markieviczs'.'

'I ...'

'Oh, don't worry about it,' he said, when he saw how embarrassed I was. 'I heard the story from a friend who lives on the estate at Lissadell. I know you're a good girl, and that Maeve is a like a wild pony, just as her mother was.'

'So you're not cross about it?'

'Not in the slightest. Now I really have to go. See you next week.'

Then he gave me a big smile and a wave and set off down the lane.

Chapter Twenty-Nine

as I'd no bicycle, I had to walk back to Lissadell like I did in the beginning, before Maeve was my friend. I went through the servants' tunnel and along the passageway to my room. Nellie was still working upstairs, and I was glad of the quiet moments to catch my breath, and think about my new life.

I needed time to work out how to tell Nellie I was leaving.

* * *

'You're back!' said Nellie twenty minutes later, pulling off her apron and running over to sit beside me on my bed. 'Wasn't the concert the most exciting thing ever? Maeve's music sent shivers down my spine, and I'll never forget Sam's songs, and Isabelle's funny

283

poem, and singing on that stage was very scary but a bit fun too and ...'

'Yes, it was all wonderful,' I said. 'And you were a true star, but ... Nellie ... there's ... something I have to say to you.'

'What?' she asked, looking up from untying her bootlaces.

'I'm leaving Lissadell.'

Nellie jumped up, looking angrier than I'd ever seen her. 'But Lady Mary and Mrs Bailey promised! They *can't* change their minds. They *can't* make you leave. I'm going to Mrs Bailey's office right now. I'm going to tell her exactly what a mistake she's making.'

I wanted to hug my shy friend, suddenly so brave, marching towards the door, with one boot on and one off.

'No,' I said. 'No one's making me leave. You see the Master came over to my house today and ...'

Nellie sat down again and listened quietly as I told her the whole story. When I finished, she didn't say

anything. Now I was scared. Leaving was what I'd always wanted, but was it going to break my friend's heart? Would she go back to being the sad, grumpy girl I'd first known?

Then she turned to me with a huge smile. 'Oh, Lily. That is the very best news,' she cried, clapping her hands.

'So you're not sad?'

'Of course, I'm a little bit sad, but mostly I'm happy for you.'

'When I first came here, you ...'

'... I was so sad and lonely I thought I might die – and that made me mean. But then you came. You taught me how to read. You found Johanna for me. You made me laugh every single day. You changed my life. Lily, you're the best friend I've ever had – and you'll still be my friend when you're living a few miles away. Nothing will ever, ever change that.'

Now Nellie was still smiling, but tears were pouring down my cheeks.

She put her arms around me and patted my back. 'You silly girl,' she soothed. 'When we thought you had to leave in disgrace that was very bad, but now everything is different. Your dream is coming true and this is a happy, happy day.'

I stopped crying and pulled away. 'Thanks, Nellie,' I said. 'You're the best.'

'And there's one more thing,' she said. 'On my days off I'm going to borrow Miss Maeve's bicycle and when you finish school in the afternoon, we will walk and laugh and go for tea like the finest of ladies.'

'You promise?'

She laughed. 'I'll visit so often you'll be sick of the very sight of me.'

Then we hugged one more time and got ready for bed. Morning wasn't far away and there was lots of cleaning and scrubbing waiting for us.

* * *

'Come.'

As I straightened my apron and turned the handle, I remembered the very first time I'd knocked on that black door. I remembered being very frightened. I remembered my sadness at leaving school and my family, and coming to live amongst strangers at Lissadell

I stood up tall. Now I was a different girl.

I stepped into Mrs Bailey's office and was surprised to see she wasn't alone.

'I'm sorry, Lady Mary,' I said. 'I can come back to talk to Mrs Bailey another time.'

'Not at all,' said Lady Mary. 'We were only preparing an order for new bedlinen, and we've just finished. You can say whatever you need to.'

'Oh!' I said, and then the words came out quickly. 'I came to say that ... there's a vacancy for an assistant teacher in my home village ... and the Master says I can have the job. That's what I've always dreamed of and I'd like to take the job ... and it starts on Monday

next week ... but I don't want to let you down and you've both been very good to me ... and ...'

Lady Mary came over, holding out her hand for me to shake. 'Lily, that is marvellous news! It was clear from your excellent work in the sewing school, and your time with Michael and Hugh, that you were born to be a teacher. The children in your new school are very lucky that you'll be joining them.'

Mrs Bailey came from behind her desk and patted my shoulder. 'I'm very happy for you, Lily. You were a good housemaid, but I know that's not what you wanted to be.'

'Thank you both,' I said. I wondered if it was polite for me to ask for the reference they'd promised me, but as usual, Lady Mary knew the right thing to do.

'I shall prepare a reference for you,' she said. 'And it will tell the truth about what an exceptional young woman you are.'

'And if you will allow me,' said Mrs Bailey, looking at her employer. 'I would like to write one also.

There's many good things I'd like to say about this girl.'

'Thank you both,' I said again.

'Can you stay and work until your day off on Saturday, Lily?' asked Lady Mary.

'Yes, of course,' I said.

'Excellent. There's a good young girl called Bessie on the estate, and her mother has approached asking for a job for her. I expect she can start in your place on Sunday.'

Outside in the passageway a bell rang. 'I'd better go,' I said.

Lady Mary walked to the door with me. 'Maeve will miss you,' she said. 'You've been a good friend to her. She is at Ardeevin – keeping her promise to work hard at her lessons – but she is due back here on Friday, so you will have a chance to say goodbye.'

'Thank you, Lady Mary,' I said. 'I'd hate to leave without telling her.'

She smiled. 'I think you two can remain friends no

matter where you are or what you do.'

Her comment made me happy, as I fetched my duster and headed up the servants' stairs.

* * *

Leaving Lissadell was what I'd always dreamed of doing, but now it was actually happening, I couldn't help feeling sad. Every time I polished the golden birds on the bannisters, I wondered if I'd ever again see anything so fine. When I fluffed up the satin covers on Lady Mary's bed, I wondered if I'd ever again touch anything so soft. When I woke to the sound of Nellie's sweet singing, I wondered if anything could ever replace it. But then I'd think of the darling children I'd be teaching, with their muddy knees and smiling faces and I knew I was a lucky girl.

* * *

'Sam? Are you here? If you are, come out because I've

to be back to turn down the beds in twenty minutes.'

It was already Thursday, and I hadn't seen Sam since the night of the concert.

I heard a rustling noise coming from one of the horse-boxes, and Sam crawled out, all red-faced and covered in straw. 'Poor Hero had a splinter on his leg, and I had to get it out.'

He stood up, closed the door, and patted the horse's head. 'You were a brave boy, weren't you? A lesser horse would have been crying for his mammy, but not you.'

I smiled. Watching Sam with the horses was a joy. He brushed off the worst of the straw, and the two of us sat on a bench in the sunshine.

'You were the star of the concert,' I said. 'Every-one's talking about what a good singer you are.'

He smiled, not seeming embarrassed by the praise. 'It was a big success,' he said. 'Lady Mary made nearly forty-two pounds for the war effort, and that's going to be such a help to our soldiers.'

'That's a lot of money,' I said, hardly able to imagine such a big sum.

'And a man came over to me after the concert, and asked me to sing in one he's giving in Rosses Point next week. There's even talk of another in Sligo Town. Can you imagine that – me on stage in such a big place? You were right, Lily. There's other ways to help the war besides fighting.'

'I'm glad you see that now,' I said, wondering if Sam's mam and dad would ever know how close their boy had come to heading off to war.

He laughed. 'But when I'm eighteen I'm still going to fight – and nothing you say will stop me.'

'I'm sure the war will be long over by then – and I won't be here at Lissadell,' I said quietly.

'How do you know? Do you …?' He stopped talking and stared at me. 'Lily? Have you got something to tell me?'

'Yes! I'm going to be a teacher! It's happening, Sam, it's really happening.'

Sam jumped up and grabbed my hands and pulled me to my feet. He danced me around in a circle, singing at the top of his voice – 'Lily is a teacher. Lily is a teacher,' over and over again until we were both dizzy and breathless and laughing like mad.

Finally, we threw ourselves back onto the bench. 'I won't see you again,' he said sadly. 'In the morning I'm going home to see my family for a few days, and won't be back until Monday. By then you'll be Miss Brennan, the nicest teacher in all of Ireland.'

We chatted for a few more minutes, and said our goodbyes.

'There's a whole new life waiting for you, Lily,' said Sam. 'And I'm very excited and happy for you – but I'll miss you too.'

'Thank you,' I said. 'I'll miss you too.' Then I hurried away, and when I turned back he gave a big wave and a cheer.

* * *

'Guess who?'

As always, I knew it was Maeve who'd crept up behind me and put her hands over my eyes. None of my servant friends had soft blister-free skin like hers.

'Maeve?' I said slowly, as if I had to think about my answer.

'Every single time!' said Maeve, stamping her foot, pretending to be angry.

I turned to face her, wishing I didn't have to tell her my news.

'Aunt Mary told me you're leaving on Monday,' she said, saving me the trouble.

'Yes. I'm going to be a teacher. Living at Lissadell and getting to know you has been so ...'

Suddenly Maeve burst into tears and threw her arms around me. 'No one will ever understand me like you do, Lily,' she sobbed into my hair. 'You always know the right things to say and do to make me feel better. I wish I could buy a house in your village and

live there and see you every single day.'

I pulled away from her and held her hands in mine. 'I don't think Gaga would be very happy about that.'

'You're probably right, and I don't think I'll run away any more. I still have one year and eleven months and two weeks and two days before I leave for boarding school – and I don't want to do anything that might change that.'

'You could visit me,' I said. 'I'll have more free time than I have here. Some days I'll help Mam with her jobs, but she won't need me every day. School finishes at half past three and it won't take me too long to tidy up and prepare for the next morning. Maybe you could ...'

'Albert will drive me,' she said. 'Any time I want. Will I come and see you on Monday afternoon at half past four?'

I smiled, loving the way my friend always had a plan. 'Monday is probably a bit soon,' I said. 'I might have to work extra-late for a few days while I'm get-

ting used to being a teacher.'

'Oh, all right. I'll leave it until the week after so. I'll write to let you know what day to expect me. Now let's get going to the beach. Mrs Bailey says you've to be back in an hour to help Nellie tidy the linen cupboard.'

I'm going to miss you, I thought as I ran out into the fresh, cold air with my wild, adventurous friend.

* * *

For once, Saturday morning almost came too quickly. After breakfast, Nellie came to the little bedroom we shared, and watched me pack up my belongings – my prayer book, my hairbrush, my nightgown, my change of clothes, and the few other things I'd got in the time I'd been at Lissadell.

'I have something for you,' she said shyly, handing me a piece of pretty blue ribbon. 'I thought you could use it to tie back your hair for work on Monday – and

maybe think of me.'

'Oh, Nellie,' I said, hugging her. 'I will think of you a hundred times a day.'

There was a small tap on the door, and some of our friends came in.

'I made you something,' said Isabelle, handing me a beautifully embroidered hanky. Johanna gave me a pretty lace collar for my best dress, and Delia and Ita gave me a card they'd made themselves, with funny drawings of all the servants. I thanked them, and then they hurried off to do their jobs.

My uniform had gone to the laundry so it would be ready for Bessie to wear. I'd already polished the black work shoes and left them under my bed, where I'd found them on my first day. I straightened the blankets one more time, and turned to Nellie.

'That's it, I suppose. Time for me to go.'

'Oh,' she said, fetching something from under her pillow. 'I nearly forgot. Sam came to the kitchen yesterday, and gave me this for you.'

It was a beautiful carving of a horse mounted on a small block of wood.

'I never had the chance to teach Sam to read,' I said sadly.

'I could do it!' said Nellie. 'I still have all the copy-books you used when you were teaching me. It would be fun and I'd like to help him.'

'Oh, Nellie,' I cried, starting to cry. 'I have such lovely friends here. Everyone is so good and kind. How can I ever …?'

Nellie came and took my hand. 'You have good friends because you *are* a good friend,' she said. 'And that will never change. Now come along. Wipe away your tears. It's time for you to go.'

So I tightened my soft blue-green shawl around my shoulders and followed Nellie out of the room.

*   *   *

In the basement passageway Mrs Bailey shook my

hand and gave me the reference she had written. 'You've been a little ray of sunshine around here, Lily,' she said. 'And we will all miss you.'

I thought she might have had a tear in her eye, but maybe it was only a speck of dust. I felt a bit choked up again too. All these goodbyes were making me sad.

'Nellie, you may stay with Lily until she leaves,' said Mrs Bailey. 'And then you can start on the family bedrooms. Next week you'll have Bessie to help you, and if she's only half as good as Lily, then she will be fine.'

'Have you said goodbye to Maeve?' asked Nellie when Mrs Bailey had hurried off to her office.

'I want to,' I said sadly. 'But she's somewhere upstairs with her family – and now that I'm not a housemaid any more, I've no business going up there. Will you please tell her I said goodbye, and that I hope to see her soon?'

'Yes of course. I can …'

'Lily? Wait.' This was Cook's voice. 'I have a few little things for your family.'

She came out of the pantry carrying the biggest basket I'd ever seen. Cook is fine and strong, and I could see it was almost too much for her.

'I've put in all the things your family like,' she said. 'And a few of your favourite custard tarts and a chicken – and anything else I could think of. Lady Mary says you may keep the basket, and the jars and things. Your mam will find a use for them.'

'Thank you, Cook,' I said. 'My family will …' I couldn't say any more as I took the basket from her and struggled not to fall over from the weight of it.

'You're welcome, child,' she said, patting my head gently before going back to the kitchen.

I followed Nellie out to the courtyard, smiling as we passed the small stone pond where little Michael had once put the seal he'd rescued. We were almost at the servants' tunnel when I heard a shriek behind me.

'Lily! How dare you leave without saying goodbye!'

I put the basket and the schoolbag onto the cobbles and turned to greet Maeve.

'Aunt Mary is upstairs,' she said. 'And she wants to see you before you go.'

She picked up the basket, groaning with the weight of it. I took my schoolbag, and Nellie and I followed Maeve inside, and up to the big marble hallway.

Lady Mary looked beautiful as usual, dressed in a blue silk dress, with matching shoes.

'This is your reference, Lily,' she said. 'It says many good things about you – and they are all true. I am happy you have the teaching job you wanted, but everyone at Lissadell will miss you very much.'

'Thank you, Lady Mary,' I said, taking the envelope and putting it safely into my schoolbag with the one from Mrs Bailey.

Now Lady Mary pointed at a large laundry bag on the chair next to her. 'I know how much you like to sew, and how your little sisters love the dresses you made for them, so I've packed up some fabric and

other things for you.'

The bag was huge! I peeked inside and saw all kinds of fabric in pinks and blues and greens – almost every colour in the rainbow. There were skeins of thread and cards of lace and ribbon and buttons.

'Oh, thank you, Lady Mary! You've always been kind to me, and I'm going to miss you very much.'

'Come along,' she said briskly, perhaps seeing that I was ready to cry. She picked up the bag of fabric and walked towards the front door. 'Your mother will be waiting. She will be so happy to have you back with her again.'

We all went down the steps and out through the porte cochère, where I realised there was a problem. My satchel was under my arm, Lady Mary handed me the laundry bag, and there was no possible way I could carry Cook's basket all the way home too.

Maeve laughed. 'I can come with you and help you to carry everything if you like.'

'That's kind of you, Maeve,' said Lady Mary. 'But

don't you have a violin lesson in an hour? Anyway, I have a better idea.' She went back inside, and I heard her calling for Mr Kilgallon.

'Just a few minutes,' she said when she returned. 'I will leave you now, Lily, as I have to speak to the nurse about the children. Thank you once again. Your time with us has been a joy.' She shook my hand and went back inside.

Nellie, Maeve and I waited – though we weren't sure what we were waiting for.

'Maybe Aunt Mary is sending one of the field workers to carry your things for you,' suggested Maeve.

'Or maybe she's having the gardener's cart sent over so you can wheel your things home,' said Nellie.

Then the Gore-Booth's beautiful shiny motor car came around the corner. It stopped beside us, and I wondered who was going out. Lady Mary was upstairs in the nursery, and Sir Josslyn was away.

Albert stepped out of the car and came towards us.

'Your car awaits, Miss Lily,' he said. 'May I help you with your bags?'

My mouth dropped open, Maeve clapped her hands and Nellie got a fit of giggles.

Albert put my bags into the car. 'Ready when you are, Miss Lily,' he said, opening the door for me.

I turned to my friends and the three of us hugged for a long time. Maeve was crying, but brave Nellie did her best to smile. I climbed into the car, and Albert put a rug over my knees, and closed the door.

'Goodbye,' I called. 'Goodbye, Maeve. Goodbye, Nellie. Come and see me soon.'

The car drove slowly down the drive, and I turned for a last look at Lissadell House, at my friends, at my old life. I was leaving like a fine lady – but being a fine lady wasn't my dream. I had always dreamed of being a teacher, and now my dream was about to come true.

A Note on the History in this Book

Maeve de Markievicz and her family were real people and the Gore-Booth family really did live in Lissadell House at the time this book is set. Though I have strayed a little from the exact truth from time to time, so the story could flow more freely, their lives were very like those described in *Lily Takes A Chance*.

Lily, Nellie, Johanna, Sam, Harry and their friends didn't really exist, but the lives they lived and the jobs they did as servants in the Big House are as accurate as I could make them. I worked very hard at researching this book, but even so, I may have made some mistakes. Try not to judge me!

Maeve de Markievicz as a girl, with her grandmother Lady Georgina (Gaga)

Schools in Ireland in Lily's Time

Lily began her teaching career in 1915. At the time, most country schools were single-storey buildings with only one or two rooms. This meant that many different age groups had to share a room. Most schools did not have a toilet that flushed. Heating was usually from an open fire, and children were often expected to bring a sod of turf to school with them for the fire. Older pupils sometimes had the job of lighting and cleaning the fire as few schools had caretakers.

In cities, children between the ages of six and fourteen were expected to attend school for at least seventy-five days a year. Children in country areas could be excused for domestic work, gathering crops

This is my great-grandfather, Daniel Curtin, 'The Master', with his wife and some of his sixteen children. He was principal of Mountcollins National School in the early twentieth century – around the time Lily would have started teaching. He was called 'The Master' to his face, and 'Dan the Goat' by his pupils (when he wasn't listening).

or helping in fisheries. At the time, some children stayed at primary school until the age of fifteen, as there was no free secondary education.

The only compulsory subjects were English and arithmetic (which we call 'maths' in primary schools today), with all other subjects optional, depending on the teachers and facilities available. (Irish was not compulsory until 1920.)

In 1916 there were still ninety-six workhouse schools in Ireland and no schools for children with additional needs.

From 1904 onwards, schools with enough pupils were allowed to appoint a Junior Assistant Mistress (JAM). These young teachers didn't need any formal teacher training once they had 'a good primary-school education'. They taught the younger classes and also taught singing, needlework, cookery and laundry to the older girls.

At the time, female teachers were paid less than males(!). In 1916, the average yearly pay for a female

teacher was 70 pounds, 2 shillings and 3 pence. (Lily would have been paid much less than this as she wasn't trained.)

Children playing outside Ballidian National School, Ballybay in County Monaghan. The girls playing 'Green grow the rushes, O' while boys do gymnastic exercises watched over by their teacher. The school where Lily taught would have been quite like this.

Further Reading

These are some of the resources I used while writing this book.

Maeve de Markievicz by Clive Scoular

Constance Markievicz by Anne Haverty

The Gore-Booths of Lissadell by Dermot James

Constance Markievicz by Joe McGowan

A Coward if I Return, a Hero if I Fall by Neil Richardson

www.lissadellhouse.com

askaboutireland.ie

cso.ie

Acknowledgements

Thanks once again to Michael O'Brien who first suggested that I write about the Gore-Booth family and Lissadell House. Michael died in 2022 before this book was published, but I hope he would have enjoyed reading Lily's latest adventure.

The Cassidy-Walsh family, the current owners of Lissadell, generously allowed me into their home and gave me lots of valuable information – thank you.

Thanks also to Ann McConnell from the INTO who gave me helpful information about JAMs.

Turn the page to see
the rest of the

Lissadell
series

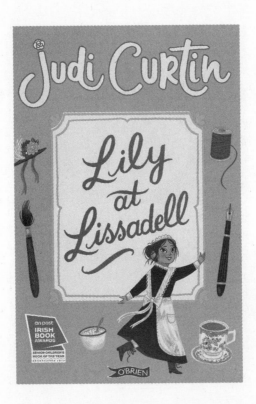

When Lily is a young teenager, the time comes for her and her friends to leave school and find work; some are emigrating to America, some going to work in shops. Lily is going into service in the Big House – Lissadell. A warm and engaging story about friendship and life in the early 20th century.

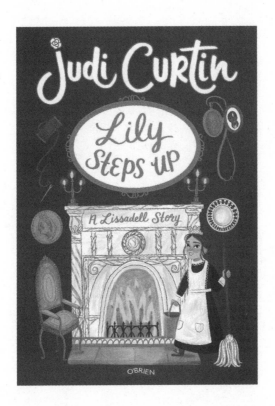

Lily and Nellie work hard as housemaids in Lissadell. And yet their days are full of friendship and fun. But Nellie is all alone in the world; she grew up in the workhouse, where she was separated from her sisters. Lily longs to help her, but how can she?

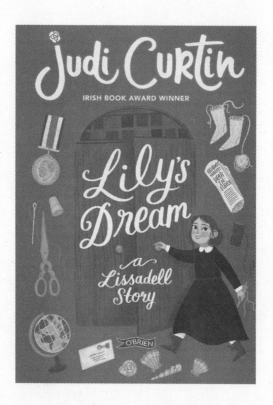

With her friendship with Maeve under strain, a war in Europe starting and uncertainty about her future, Lily needs all her wits about her!